'You know, y... better for y... stay here?'

'I have my reasons.'

He studied her for a long moment, his gaze causing her to dread what he'd say next. 'The same reasons that made you cut and run from Rexford?'

She swallowed hard. 'No—not really. I've told you why I did that.'

He clearly dismissed that as an answer unworthy of comment. 'I thought it might be the same reason that ensures you are never able to accept an invitation because you don't have a free evening?'

Flustered, she shrugged, but didn't speak in case her voice let her down.

'Do you have other commitments, Jenny?'

'Commitments? Like what?' She felt the colour draining from her face.

'Looking after your child, for instance?'

Although a Lancastrian by birth, **Sheila Danton** has now settled in the West Country with her husband. Her nursing career, which took her to many parts of England, left her with 'itchy feet' that she indulges by travelling both at home and abroad. She uses her trips to discover new settings for her books, and also to visit their three grown-up children, who have flown the nest in different directions.

Recent titles by the same author:

GOOD HUSBAND MATERIAL
THE PATIENT LOVER

THE NURSE'S SECRET CHILD

BY
SHEILA DANTON

MILLS & BOON®

All the characters in this book have no existence outside the imagination of the author, and have no relation whatsoever to anyone bearing the same name or names. They are not even distantly inspired by any individual known or unknown to the author, and all the incidents are pure invention.

First published in Great Britain 2002
Harlequin Mills & Boon Limited,
Eton House, 18-24 Paradise Road, Richmond, Surrey TW9 1SR

© Sheila Danton 2002

ISBN 0 263 83092 6

Set in Times Roman 10½ on 12 pt.
03-0902-47352

Printed and bound in Spain
by Litografía Rosés, S.A., Barcelona

CHAPTER ONE

'I'VE just been introduced to the new consultant,' Rosie, the recently arrived house officer, told Sister Jenny Stalham excitedly. 'Apparently he's a bit of a high-flyer so they're lucky to get him. In fact, they can't believe he wanted to come here.'

'About time they got someone half-decent. What's he called?'

'Max. And he made *max*imum impact on me!'

Jenny looked at her irrepressible colleague, carefully hiding the mixed emotions she always felt whenever she heard that particular name. 'Max what?'

'I've forgotten.' Rosie was generally vague about anything not connected with work. 'Or perhaps I wasn't listening. Not surprising, really. He's drop-dead gorgeous. Enough to make you forget your own name.'

Jenny groaned inwardly, then told herself it couldn't possibly be Max Field. His carefully worked out career plan hadn't included a hospital in this part of the world.

'I remember now. Field, it was. Max Field,' gabbled Rosie, immediately dashing Jenny's optimism. 'I expect he'll be along to meet you soon.'

Jenny stared at her wordlessly. What on earth was he doing here?

'You all right, Jen?' Rosie asked. 'You look a bit peaky.'

'Not surprising,' she muttered beneath her breath. She'd never expected to see the father of her child again. Not that she hadn't once dreamed she might come across him in the course of her work, but certainly not in the North of England.

For once Rosie's intuition kicked in. 'You know him, don't you?'

'I'm afraid so. I—I used to work with him.'

Rosie looked sombre. 'Oh, dear! Is he that bad to work with? And I thought he seemed very pleasant back there…'

'He is. Don't get me wrong. It's just—'

'Yes?' Rosie prompted, eager for gossip.

'Me being silly,' Jenny improvised hurriedly. 'Call it a personality clash, if you like.'

'You?' Rosie was scornful. 'I can't believe that. You get on with everybody.'

'I suppose I never really got to know him. We only worked together for a short time.'

She could see Rosie didn't believe her, but in fact it was the truth. She'd left Rexford Hospital two months to the day after he'd taken up his appointment there.

It had been lust, not love, at first sight. She'd managed to convince herself of that, at least. Lust that had led them to leap into bed together only three weeks into their burgeoning relationship—and she had paid for it with the job she had been working towards for seven years.

'Get a move on, Rosie. Customer waiting time's increasing fast.' She chivvied the house officer more sharply than usual. 'I'll update the information board.'

She checked the occupancy of each cubicle in the busy Accident and Emergency department and allocated staff where necessary, but as soon as she could she made her way to the office to give herself a moment's breather. It was a mistake. It must be. Same name, good-looking, but a different person. The Max Field she knew had his career all mapped out—knew exactly which hospitals he was going to move on to. Catonbury certainly wasn't one of them.

It was some time later that she knew she was wrong. She'd just emerged from a harrowing chat with two desperately worried parents when she heard his unmistakably deep voice. 'Who's in charge today?'

Fran, the young care assistant assigned to the department only that week, didn't speak, but pointed towards Jenny.

His step didn't falter.

'Could I speak to you in your office, Sister?'

Surprised by his formality, Jenny stole a glance at his face and saw his eyes were conveying something very different.

Experiencing a sudden reminder of the physical effect he could produce in her, she panicked and looked around. 'It's—er not a good time at the moment.' She gestured hopelessly towards the over-full waiting area, then turned towards Fran and said, 'Could you take a cup of tea to the couple in there? But tread carefully. Their child has suspected meningitis, so they're very upset.'

'OK, I'll try later,' he declared, in a tone that seemed to Jenny more of a threat than a promise.

She didn't move as she watched his retreating back disappear round the corner. Nothing had changed about him. Still the same dark, dark hair, bordering on black. Perhaps one or two more laugh lines around his intense blue eyes. Eyes such a dark blue that they were nearly brown. Eyes she was reminded of every day.

She shook herself and tried to push all thoughts of him to the back of her mind. But several nagging queries remained. What was he doing here, and why hadn't Andy or Dan formally introduced the new consultant before letting him loose in the department? Or was his visit un-official?

That thought sent an icy shiver through her veins and a momentary panic gripped her that he might have discovered she had a son. But she was reassured by the thought that that was well-nigh impossible.

Rosie raced past on her way to the X-ray screen and called over her shoulder, 'Is he the one you know?'

Jenny nodded ruefully, ''fraid so.' Grateful for Rosie's early warning, which had probably prevented her from making a complete fool of herself when she saw him, she added with a reassuring grin, 'I'm not sure he recognised me, though, so hopefully it'll be a fresh start. And he is good at his job. One of the best. I'm looking forward to working with him again.'

Rosie's raised eyebrow told Jenny that she'd believe that when she saw it—and no wonder, after what she'd blurted out earlier.

Finding everything under control in the major injuries end of the department, she checked that the paediatric team had taken control of the youngster with suspected meningitis, and discovered he was just about to be moved up to the children's ward.

After explaining to his worried parents what was happening, and reassuring them as much as she could, she immersed herself in what she loved best: the hands-on work of the department alongside the rest of her staff. Within an hour the backlog was clearing, and she called one of the low-priority cases.

'Mr James?'

He was clearly very unhappy. 'I've been waiting three and a half hours, you know.' He stomped beside her to the treatment area.

Jenny read through his card, then nodded towards the

'approximate waiting time' indicator. 'I am sorry, but you were advised by the triage nurse that this wasn't a life-threatening injury, and I'm afraid we have to deal with the most serious cases first. Now, tell me what happened.'

'I was working on the car and I reached up to look for a spanner and gashed my arm on the side of the bonnet.' He pointed to the dressing Annette, the triage nurse that day, had put over the area. Relief that someone was at last taking an interest in his injury had dispelled his anger for the time being.

Jenny pulled on a pair of rubber gloves and warned him, 'I'm just going to remove this.' She peeled the dressing back to reveal his wound. 'That's not bad at all. I'll clean it up and get the doctor to check it. Flesh wounds always bleed more than others, and often seem worse than they really are. When did you last have a tetanus injection?'

'No idea. Can't remember ever letting anyone near me with a needle. Don't need one, do I?'

'Probably. You haven't been abroad and needed vaccinations?'

'Me? You must be joking. Why do you think I'm doing my own car repairs? Skint, I am. Completely skint.'

'The doctor will probably advise you to have one. It covers you for ten years, and it's better than getting lockjaw. Especially if you're into a lot of do-it-yourself.'

'Hmph.'

As she left the cubicle she raised an eyebrow towards Rosie, who grinned and, taking the card, said, 'I heard the end of that.'

'Another one complaining about the delay. Annette had advised him it might have been easier to go to his GP, but he chose to stay and wait.'

'I suppose it's panic when something like that happens. They want instant service and think only we can give it.'

Jenny was about to call the next person through when Max suddenly strode back into the department. She'd forgotten all about him as she worked, and the sight of him set her heart thudding so unevenly that she had to surreptitiously grab the desk beside her for support.

'Quieter now.'

Unsure if it was a statement or a question, she nodded. 'We had three heavy cases one after the other, but touch wood…'

He nodded his understanding. 'So you could spare me a moment?'

She'd have to some time. 'I'll be in the office if you need me,' she told Leanne, who had been clearing the backlog beside her, then led the way to her office.

He followed her in and closed the door.

'It's good to see you again, Jenny.'

'And you…' She hesitated, wanting to know why he was there, but scared that she might give away too much. She was unable to meet his eyes. 'It must be three years…'

'Nearer four, I'd say. Why?'

She frowned as she switched her kettle on. 'Why four years? It just is, I suppose. Rosie—Dr Harben—tells me you're our new consultant. I'm surprised you've changed your mind about working in a hospital like this.'

'Changed my mind?'

'I was under the impression that you thought only the top London hospitals would look good on your CV.'

There was no response, so she turned away from the kettle and saw he was regarding her steadily.

Unable to stand the silence, she asked, 'Coffee? Or tea?'

'Coffee. Black. No sugar.'

'Of course. I remember now.' She filled two mugs and handed him one, then reluctantly sat down, but moved her chair so she wasn't in his direct line of vision.

'Thanks for this.'

'Have you started work already? I thought Andy Moss would have introduced you to the department first. I mean, it's all right, as I know you, but if I'd been off duty you might have been thrown out as an impostor.' She gave a hesitant laugh.

'I'm sure the good manager has better things to do with his time—especially as I don't officially start work until tomorrow. I thought you might have time to show an old friend around before that.'

Old friend. Was that how he thought of her? 'Yes. Well…' Jenny compressed her lips. 'You saw how it was, and how it is now. It's hard to suggest a good time.'

'Not the present?'

'I can't leave the department.'

'It'll do for a start. *After* you've answered that "why".'

'Why what?' she queried as innocently as she could, still refusing to meet his gaze.

'Why you are in this godforsaken hole. Why you left Rexford so abruptly. Why you didn't let me know you were going. Why—'

She interrupted him with a raised hand. 'Hold on. That's enough or I'll forget what you asked.' The thought struck her that he sounded just like Jamie, responding to every answer she gave with 'Why?'. Although she really hadn't provided Max with any answers as yet, and didn't intend to. At least not the truth.

'OK, we'll go through them one by one. First.' He struck one index finger with the other. 'Why did you run off three and a half years ago?'

'I didn't "run off", as you put it. I needed a job.'

'You had one.'

'Not after that interview.'

'You could have stayed until you found something better.'

'I certainly could not. I was ashamed and humiliated. The whole of Rexford Hospital knew—'

'It would have been a five-day wonder.'

'I couldn't stay and work with the person they did appoint. She wasn't even as qualified—'

'So why didn't you let me know what you were doing?' His interruption was brusque. He clearly wanted answers and wanted them fast.

'I—I did try…' Again she averted her eyes to hide the hurt she'd felt at his not returning her calls. 'It seemed you were busy elsewhere at the time.'

He moved towards her and grasped her right arm, setting the nerves under her skin jumping. She looked up, and quickly away again.

'What are you suggesting?' he rasped.

'I'm merely stating the truth, Max. Incidentally, how is Clare?' That should make it clear to him that she knew only too well whom he'd been busy with!

'Very well, considering what she went through with the chemotherapy. And she was one of the lucky ones.'

'I can imagine.' At his confirmation that Clare was still on the scene. She attempted to escape his hold and said, 'I would appreciate it if you'd let go of my arm.'

When he didn't move, she muttered, 'Do you want a quick tour of the department or not? Because I have plenty else to do.'

He released her with an exasperated gesture. 'I'm sure you do. But yes, I would be grateful if you could spare me the time for a lightning visit to the important parts.'

He touched his forelock in a humorous gesture of gratitude and she muttered, 'Always the joker. You haven't changed.'

His only answer was the cynical lift of an eyebrow.

Jenny ignored it. 'We'll go to the major end first.' As they prepared to leave her office she tried to prompt him into revealing why he was at Catonbury. 'You must have been surprised to find you'd be working with me.'

'I knew this was the area you'd moved to, and vaguely wondered if we might bump into one another, but I certainly didn't expect to find you still here. However, when I told one of the locums I was working with that I'd got this post he mentioned working here with someone who'd been at Rexford. I put two and two together and guessed it must be you.'

'You had an advantage over me, then.' Determined he shouldn't think it important to her, she led the way briskly into the first resuscitation room. 'This is Lisa. She's often in charge when I'm not on duty.'

They shook hands and Jenny explained it was just a quick orientation tour for the new consultant. She sensed Lisa and a couple of the other girls in the room follow him with their eyes as he poked around. Nothing new in that, she thought sourly. His startling looks combined with the fancy waistcoats he always wore to house his grandfather's fob watch claimed every female's attention, especially with his dark hair cut shorter than she recalled, taming the unruly waves that had been such a challenge for him to control.

He turned and saw her studying him. His sudden dazzling smile caught her unawares, demolishing all her efforts to deny the potency of his attraction. In that instant she knew her resolve to pretend their affair had never happened had failed. This feeling in her chest wasn't lust.

It was love. Pure and simple. She still loved him, and wanted him, and it was going to be pure hell working so closely with him knowing he didn't feel the same.

'Don't you want to know which locum it was?'

Struggling to regain control of her emotions, she shrugged. 'I don't suppose I'll even remember the name. We get so many. Did you want to tell me?'

He shook his head. 'It's not important.'

So why was he making such a song and dance about it? 'That's what I thought.' He really was behaving oddly. First of all coming to work at a hospital north of Watford, which he had told her he would never do, then arriving in the department a day early and all the time pushing her for answers—as if he cared. Although she had believed it once, she now knew better.

To counteract the unease he was generating within her, she assumed her most businesslike manner. 'We'll take a quick look at the minor end now, if that's OK?' Before they could make a move to do so the relative quiet of the department was shattered as a bellowing girl was trolleyed into the majors end. Rosie joined the team gathering round the girl.

The green-clad paramedic gave the details unemotionally and concisely. 'Female. Early twenties. Cyclist. Hit by car. Protesting at coming here rather than badly hurt.'

'Name?' Rosie asked.

'Won't say.' The paramedic rolled his eyes and shook his head. 'Think she could be a student.'

Jenny leaned over the girl and, taking her hand, said gently, 'The sooner you co-operate with us, the sooner you'll be on your way.'

The noise stopped abruptly. 'Get rid of that chauvinist first.' The girl nodded towards the ambulanceman. 'And do something about my bike. *If* it hasn't been stolen already.'

Helping to position the girl comfortably onto the couch in one of the cubicles, Jenny heard the paramedic say, 'I've already told you that the police were securing it when we left. All right if I dash? There's another call.'

'Like hell they were…' The girl was incensed.

Max glanced at the various monitors that were now in place and raised an eyebrow at Jenny who, sensing they would get no co-operation from the girl while the paramedic was still there, nodded. 'That's fine. We can take it from here.'

The moment the doors swung closed behind him the patient visibly relaxed.

Jenny handed the observation chart to Max and asked, 'What's your name?'

'Laura Watson.'

'Where does it hurt, Laura?'

'I've grazed my knee and elbow, but I can see to those myself. Honestly, there was no need for all this fuss.'

'We can take a look at those in a minute,' Rosie, who had been checking Laura from head to toe, held up the cycling helmet that was at the foot of the trolley. 'At least this protected your head, but it took a battering. You'll need to get a new one.'

'*If* I've still got a bike. That silly old fool wouldn't listen to anything I said. Treated me like an idiot and implied a female shouldn't be riding a bike on the main road.'

'I wondered what he'd done to cause such a violent reaction,' Max muttered quietly as Rosie asked Laura about the actual blow to her head.

Eventually satisfied, she told the girl, 'There's no damage as far as I can see. We'll get you cleaned up and then ask Reception to trace where your bike is now. When did you last have a tetanus injection, by the way?'

'Would you believe last month? My new GP insisted.'

'Great. Just don't forget the new helmet. This one probably saved your life.'

Max followed Jenny out of the area and they continued their tour. 'Competent woman, that HO.'

Despite experiencing an unexpected flicker of jealousy, Jenny had to agree. 'She's only been here a short time, but we're impressed.'

'Worked in A & E before?'

'Six months. She wants to specialise.'

'In A & E?'

'That's what she says at the moment. Better watch your back,' Jenny laughed.

'Incredible,' Max breathed.

Jenny swung round to look at him. 'Why? Think she won't make it, do you?' she snapped accusingly.

'The thought never crossed my mind. Actually, I was referring to you. That's the first time you've laughed today. I was beginning to wonder where all the fun had gone.'

Taken completely by surprise, Jenny felt the colour flare in her cheeks. 'Still there when it's appropriate,' she told him huffily.

He raised his eyebrow. 'Ooh. Touchy, aren't we? I wonder why?'

Ignoring his comment, she stopped at the large board which depicted where each of the current patients was to be found. Annette was in the process of updating it. 'These are our treatment cubicles.' She briefly explained how their system worked, but then, sure he wasn't listening properly, told him, 'I hope you've seen all you need to because I'm running out of time.'

'I'm sorry to have delayed you,' he murmured silkily. 'I too have things to catch up on. What are you doing tonight?'

'Pardon?'

'Are you free this evening?'

Surely he wasn't expecting her to resume a relationship that had existed for such a short time several years before? Especially as she knew Clare wasn't the platonic chum he had once maintained. 'I'm afraid not…'

'I thought you wouldn't be.' He nodded thoughtfully. 'See you in the morning.' He turned and walked out of the department without another word.

Puzzled, Jenny watched him until he went out of sight, then, after checking with Annette that she was coping, made her way through the department back to her office, trying to work out if his last remark meant he was expecting more of her than she was prepared to give.

Rosie popped her head round the door a moment later. 'He seems all right.'

'I guess so, but I'm still not sure why he was here today. I don't believe he was listening to a word I had to say, and what he saw of the department is not going to be of much help to him when he starts work tomorrow.'

'Perhaps he was trying to discover how *you* felt about *him* working here!'

Her words made Jenny think. She hadn't looked at it from his point of view. She had been too wrapped up in her own fears, believing that he had come for some devious reason she couldn't fathom. His move might be quite innocent. And yet…it just didn't fit with what she knew about him and his ambition.

She groaned. There must be hundreds of accident and emergency departments in the country, so when he had decided to abandon his original career plan why had he chosen this one? It must have been a deliberate move on his part. After all he had admitted he knew she had moved to this area. But why would he want to come when he had made it so clear she meant nothing to him?

She presumed he must now be married, or soon would be, to Clare. So all he could want from her was another quick fling. If that was the case he could just think again. The thought of how gullible she'd been in the past still caused her pain, and it must have shown on her face.

'I can see that's made you stop and think.' Rosie slipped a comforting arm around her shoulder. 'Don't worry about it. He's my boss, not yours. Let's go and have a bite of lunch and forget about him.'

'I'll sort the others out, then join you,' Jenny told her.

As she walked down to the canteen the directorate's administrative assistant joined her. 'Hi, Jenny. Have you heard about your new consultant?'

'Max?' She nodded. 'I worked with him at Rexford, so he came to see me this morning. You did well to entice him here.'

Dan Turner raised an eyebrow smugly. 'Andy and I could hardly believe it when we read his application form. I must confess I did wonder if he perhaps had a complaint pending against him, but it seems I maligned him.'

'Did he—did he give any reason for applying?'

'He considers it a stepping stone in his career.'

'Catonbury? Never!'

Dan's frown was fleeting, but Jenny didn't miss it. 'Do you know something we don't?'

Wishing she hadn't broached the subject, she laughed and shook her head. 'Sorry to disappoint you, but as far as I know there are no skeletons in his cupboard as far as work's concerned.' Only in his private life, and Dan wouldn't be interested in those.

'Thank goodness for that.' He pushed open the door of the canteen to discover the object of their conversation just ahead of them in the queue.

'Your ears must be burning, Max.'

He turned and gave them both a teasing smile. 'You're not complaining about me already, Jenny? Are you?'

To her intense irritation she felt an unaccustomed heat rise in her cheeks for a second time that morning, despite knowing he wasn't serious.

'Not yet, but I'm working on it.' His dry sense of humour had been one of his biggest attractions for her, and, having always tried to give as good as she got, she decided now wasn't the time to change.

Dan looked from one to the other and, completely missing the tongue-in-cheek nature of their exchange, rushed in to reassure Catonbury's prize catch. 'Actually, she was being very complimentary about you. Anyway, I've just seen someone I need to have a word with, so I'll see you later.'

'I'm pleased to hear it,' Max told Jenny gravely as Dan sped off. 'And to show you how much I appreciate it, I'll treat you to lunch, Jen.'

'It's Jenny, these days, and I'm only having a quick coffee.' She was actually starving, but a cosy chat over lunch was something she wanted to avoid at all costs.

He turned and surveyed her from head to toe before murmuring, 'I can't see any need for you to cut your intake of food, and after the way you've been rushing about that's not enough. What are you going to have?'

Unable to prevent herself flushing at the indirect compliment, she snapped, 'I told you—'

'And I insist you eat something. Now, what's it to be?'

Reluctantly she chose the vegetable lasagne.

He ordered two portions and coffee, and carried the tray

to an empty table for two. When he placed the food in front of her she thanked him and started to eat, keeping her eyes fixed on her plate.

'The food seems OK here.'

She nodded, but still didn't look up.

'Are you sulking because I've made you eat?'

'I'm not sulking,' she retorted, stealing a glance at his face in time to see an expression of disbelief.

'You've changed, Jenny. Why?'

She shrugged. 'I've grown up.' She pushed her barely touched meal away and swallowed her coffee. 'Thanks again for lunch. I must get back to the department now.'

'You'll do your digestion no good, eating at that rate,' he told her as she left.

'Maybe not, but it'll do wonders for my peace of mind if I can avoid your company,' she muttered to herself as she climbed the stairs two at a time.

CHAPTER TWO

IT WAS a relief when her shift came to an end that day and she could get right away from the hospital.

'Hi, Mum. I'm home.'

Jamie came running down the hall towards her, followed by his grandmother. Seeing the exhaustion on her mother's face, Jenny felt a wrenching pang of guilt. Her mother shouldn't have a child to contend with at her age. Jamie was at the stage where he was busy, busy, busy—every moment of the day—and it looked as if it was becoming too much for her mother.

Resolving to put him into nursery school for an extra day, Jenny swung Jamie up into her arms and gave him a kiss.

'Your turn for a rest,' she told her mother. 'I'll make you some tea.'

Jamie was chattering into her ear, telling her all he had done and wanting her to go and look at something.

'You go with him. I'll put the kettle on.'

'No, you sit down. I'll do it.' Jenny shot her mother a worried glance as she ushered her into the living room and went out to the kitchen to make the tea. Jamie trotted out to the kitchen with her, still talking and producing various items for her to inspect, and when she took the tea into the living room and sat down, he settled on her lap, hoping to get one of the biscuits Jenny had put out to revive her mother's flagging energy.

'Everything all right, dear?' Audrey Stalham asked as Jenny passed the plate of biscuits.

'Yep.'

'You seem—well—a bit strung up. Bad day, was it?'

'I'm worried about you, Mum. Jamie's too much for you. I'll see if I can increase his days at the nursery. Give you a break.'

'He's fine here. You don't need to do that.'

'It won't be for too long.'

'Are you sure that's all you've got on your mind? You do seem a bit preoccupied this evening.'

Aware her mother could be too perceptive at times, she sought for an explanation that would satisfy her. 'We've another consultant starting tomorrow. I don't know where I am with all these changes in staff.'

'What happened to the last one? It doesn't seem five minutes since you were worrying about him arriving.'

'It isn't. Although Catonbury's a good hospital, its situation means it doesn't attract the kind of doctors who are likely to stay put any longer than absolutely necessary.'

'It's a pity you couldn't have stayed where you were. You were happy at Rexford, weren't you?'

'I was, but it was time to move on whether I'd had Jamie or not. It's been wonderful to have your support. You do a wonderful job with him. But now we start looking after you. I'm going to treat you to a meal this evening.'

Her mother looked puzzled. 'We can't leave him…'

'I'm cooking. I only hope it *will* be a treat.'

'Of course it will, love. You're a good cook.'

'You flatterer. I'm just going to change and play with Jamie for a while. You go in and close the door and put your feet up.'

When Jenny's father had died, just a couple of months before Jamie was born, her mother had insisted she move into the granny flat attached to the house they'd always lived in. 'You'll need the room. I won't,' she'd insisted. 'And the house will be yours one day. Don't argue. My mind's made up.'

It had worked well. She often left the door open and Jamie pattered between the two of them. But not today. Jenny was determined her mother was going to rest.

Once Jamie was settled in bed, and her mother had enjoyed the trout she'd cooked for their supper, Jenny cleared away the dirty dishes then ran a bath. She could soak and think uninterrupted in the soothing aqua bathroom.

The first thing she tried to puzzle out was what Max was doing at Catonbury. She had been sure he would be at one of the biggest London hospitals by this time, so what was he playing at? She couldn't believe he was trying to find her—which was the only explanation she had come up with so far. Why would he bother now? If he had cared anything at all for her, he would have rung to commiserate over that disastrous interview.

The memory of it still haunted her dreams. Just two hours before she'd been interviewed for the position of Sister in Charge of Rexford Accident and Emergency Department, the pregnancy predictor strip had brutally confirmed what she'd already known.

She still went alternately hot and cold as she recalled how she had bungled both the question-and-answer session and the presentation. But all she'd think about was how Max Field, the high-flying departmental registrar, would react when she told him he was about to be a father. She had panicked and forgotten her carefully prepared replies.

In their short time together he had made it clear that a family didn't figure in his immediate plans, and, despite their heated affair, she'd soon discovered neither did she. She had been nothing more than a useful stopgap while he was in Rexford.

So she had taken all the leave owing to her and left before he returned from the compassionate leave he had taken when the girlfriend he had assured Jenny was purely platonic had developed lymphatic cancer.

Until he had appeared that morning she'd been sure she had done the right thing. She had even convinced herself that she'd never really loved him. Now she wasn't so sure. Just one glimpse of him had set her heart racing precariously.

She had come to no conclusion by the time she climbed out of the bath. Probably because there was no logical conclusion to come to—and she didn't want to stay in the water long enough to come out looking like a prune.

One thing she *was* sure about. He wasn't going to find out that Jamie was his son. Or even that she had a son, if she could help it. Thank goodness his existence wasn't common knowledge at the hospital—she had thought it safer that way.

Her mother was watching television in bed and Jamie was sleeping the exhausted sleep of the innocent, so she decided to try and do the same. It had been a difficult day and there would be another tomorrow *and* each day after that. Until she learnt to cope with working alongside the one man she had ever loved.

The accident and emergency department was eerily quiet when Jenny arrived on duty the next morning, and she was surprised to see Max already there, chatting with her night staff.

'It's been like this all night.' Donna leapt to her feet defensively. 'I've never known time drag like it. If it goes on I'll be glad to be back on days.'

'Make the most of it.' Max grinned, resting an arm on her shoulder. 'Tonight will probably be horrendous.'

Donna giggled and nodded as she quickly gathered her report papers to hand over to Jenny.

Suspicious as to what Max might have been saying to produce such a reaction in the normally dour Donna, Jenny took the reports distractedly before saying to Max, 'Like at Rexford, the full-time nursing staff work a rota which includes day and night shifts. The part-timers usually work one or the other.'

Max nodded and murmured, 'Your doing?'

'My doing?'

'Introducing the same systems of work as we had at Rexford? I was looking at the procedure sheets and several of them are identical.'

'Isn't that what experience is all about?' Jenny snapped. 'Incorporating the best—?'

'Hey! I wasn't criticising.'

'You could have fooled me.' She made her way through to her office and was pleased to note that he followed her without a backward glance at the night staff.

While she attended to her urgent paperwork he idly flipped through the reports.

Just after nine, Andy Moss walked into the department. 'I gather you've already met our new consultant.'

'We worked together briefly in the past,' Jenny told him, intending to let Max know as soon as possible that he didn't mean anything more to her than that.

'Hey! It wasn't as brief as all that,' he demurred, pretending to be hurt.

'I suppose it *was* all of two months,' she murmured innocently.

'Ah! I didn't think you could have forgotten me so easily.' His eyes met hers and she felt the probing heat of his gaze as he sought to remind her of just what their relationship had been.

She wished she could tell him it wasn't necessary. She hadn't forgotten a single thing about it.

'He's had a good effect on the department already,' she joked in an attempt to cover her feelings. 'I've never known it as quiet as this.'

'Are you suggesting I've frightened all your patients away?' Max murmured with an amused grin.

'Nothing could have been further from my mind,' she told him smoothly, 'but it means I can give you a comprehensive tour of the department without interruption.'

'Er—I'll leave you to it, then. If that's OK?' Andy had been watching the exchange between them and was clearly unsure whether he ought to stay or go.

'That's fine, Andy. I'm sure you've plenty else to be getting on with. Thanks for all your help so far.'

The manager nodded and scurried away. Max pushed the door closed behind him, then settled in the chair to the side of Jenny's desk.

'Right.'

'What would you like first? A run down of the staff, or…?'

'To find out what's happening in your life these days.'

'Max…' She hesitated. 'I don't think that is going to be of any help to either of us. We could be inundated with patients at any moment and you'd be pushed in at the deep end without…'

'Jen—Jenny, you showed me enough of the department yesterday to enable me to cope with the biggest emergency. I'm not exactly a raw recruit to A & E, and—'

'You may know what you're doing, Max, but surely it would be better if you knew which staff members can be relied on for what.'

'OK. You win. Let's do the tour and meet the locals.'

Exasperated, she led the way from the office. The trouble was, she knew him too well. His flippant comments were designed to lull her into believing nothing had changed between them.

But if he expected her to resume their affair where it had left off he could think again. When his mother had told her he would be marrying Clare as soon as she was well enough she'd realised what a fool he'd made of her, and she certainly didn't want to repeat it any more than she wanted to run from yet another job to escape him.

In any case, Catonbury was where she needed to stay for the foreseeable future—close to her mother and Jamie's nursery school.

So the only way she could survive working with him was to forget everything that had happened between them and treat him as a virtual stranger. Something his behaviour so far told her he wasn't likely to be happy about.

'This is…' She turned to introduce him to Leanne, only to discover he had stopped to confer with Rosie about the patient she was treating. While he was doing so, she checked the information on the board was up to date.

Their tour was almost at an end when Rosie beckoned them over urgently. 'Emergency on the way in. Severe abdominal pain. Young Asian woman. Collapsed in the street. Her sister has told him they both have sickle cell disease and she's seen a cousin suffer a similar attack.'

Max nodded and frowned. 'Sounds like she's in crisis. Have you dealt with one before?'

Rosie shook her head. 'I saw a few cases who came in for check-up when I was training.' She frowned. 'I don't know that I understand what you mean by "crisis."'

'Severe pain is often caused by small blood vessels becoming blocked with the sickle-shaped red blood cells.

And you can take it from me, it's excruciating. So, for a start she needs immediate pain relief and an infusion set up—how close are they?'

'Sounds like them arriving now.'

'Alert the medics, Jenny, and while you're about it see if they have a bed if we need it. I'll leave the infusion to you, Rosie, and we'll need access for blood tests and drug administration.'

'Oxygen saturation only seventy-eight per cent,' the leading paramedic announced, heading straight for the re-suscitation area.

Annette indicated an empty bay and helped to guide the trolley through. 'Let's get her off this trolley. Do we know her name?'

'Anya.'

'We're just going to move you off the trolley, Anya. On my count,' Max told them. 'One, two, three.'

'Another blanket and pain relief,' he ordered, once she was settled. 'Unless you've given her some?'

The paramedic shook his head.

'Are you Anya's sister?' Max asked the young girl in the doorway. At her nod he said, 'She's not pregnant?'

The patient pushed off her oxygen mask and spoke for the first time. 'No. I am not.' Suddenly she burst into tears.

Jenny slipped an arm around the girl's shoulder. 'It's OK, Anya. We just want to make sure it's safe to give you the drugs.'

Max frowned. 'Any medical history we should know about?' he asked the patient's sister. 'Or allergies?'

'Just the sickle cell.'

'Anything like this before?' While he spoke he was drawing up the pain-relieving drug.

'No. She's always been fine. That's probably why the ambulance man wouldn't believe us.'

'About what?' he queried absently.

'About what was wrong—the sickle cell…' She didn't finish the sentence and Jenny, seeing how upset she was becoming, suggested Fran take Anya's sister to the visitors' room.

'I'll start antibiotics as soon as you've taken blood for culture,' Max told Rosie. 'Do we have our own haematologist?'

'Already contacted, and luckily doing a clinic here today. He'll be up shortly,' said Jenny.

'Are you on the books here?' Max addressed Anya, who managed a small nod.

'Mr Renshaw?' Jenny queried.

Another nod.

'Good. He's here now.'

Max looked up and introduced himself to the young consultant who was approaching, a set of well-thumbed notes in hand. 'I believe you know Anya?'

Giles Renshaw smiled ruefully. 'She's done very well up to now.' He turned to the girl and told her, 'But this time I'm afraid we'll have to admit you, Anya.'

'I've checked, and there's a bed she can have on G ward.' Jenny completed updating the chart she'd created for Anya and handed it to him. 'This is what we've done so far.'

Scanning the chart, Giles nodded. 'The sooner we get you into a bed the better, Anya. We'll soon have you up and about again.'

Anya managed a small smile that made clear her complete trust in the consultant.

'I'll take over now. Thanks for what you've done so

far. Good to have someone on board who knows about these things.'

Max moved aside to give him more room. 'I've just been lucky. I've had some experience of genetic disorders such as this.'

'For my patients' sake, then, I hope you're here for a long stay.' Giles Renshaw chuckled. 'And for mine!'

Jenny asked Leanne to go up to the ward with them and after wishing Anya a quick recovery she went in search of the patient's sister.

Max followed her and waited until Jenny had explained what was happening. Then he probed gently, 'You say the ambulance man didn't believe you when you told him about the sickle cell disease?'

The girl shook her head, tears rising in her eyes once again. 'He was quite unpleasant about it. Insisted it must be something else.'

Max rested a hand on her shoulder. 'I'm sorry about that. Your sister has enough to contend with at the moment without that. Tell her to try and forget all about it.'

'It's not that easy…'

Max rested a hand on her shoulder. 'For you, either. I can see that.'

The girl wiped away an escaping tear, but managed a watery smile. 'How is my sister?'

'Anya has been admitted to G ward,' Jenny told her gently, 'under Mr Renshaw's care. Fran will take you up there now. I expect you know him as well as she does?'

'Yep. We both attend his clinic regularly. Thanks for everything, Sister. And you, too, Doctor.'

Jenny smiled her acknowledgement before calling through the next patient from the overcrowded waiting area. As she worked to treat one after another the morning flew by, and she found herself working contentedly alongside Max in a way she'd thought would no longer be possible. They'd always made a good team, at times reading one another's minds about the needs of a patient, and both appeared to have slipped back into their slick routine.

However, the moment there was a lull Max followed her into the office and demanded, 'What is it with this ambulance chap? That's the second complaint I've heard in two days. How many more have there been?'

'Patrick, you mean?' She frowned. 'I've been here three years and I'd have said he's one of the best paramedics we have.'

Max raised his eyebrows. 'God help the patients if the others are worse than him. Is he married?'

'He is, but—'

'But what?'

'I don't know.' She sighed. 'He said something the other day that made me think all wasn't well at home. But when I asked him how Sarah was, he muttered, "Same as usual," and took himself off before I could ask anything more.'

'You know him quite well, then? How about tackling him about upsetting Anya and her sister.'

'If the opportunity arises, I will. But I'm not his employer—'

'So it should be better coming from you.'

'Maybe, but perhaps we're making a mountain out of a molehill. Perhaps Anya and her sister live a very sheltered life.'

'What about the cyclist? He managed to upset her, too.'

'OK. I take your point.'

He sighed deeply. 'Don't you find the work here limiting? Wouldn't you prefer to be in a less parochial place. Somewhere more like Rexford?'

'I'm enjoying my time here.'

'Have you thought about moving on?'

What did it matter to him? Was he trying to provoke her into telling him more than she wanted to? It was almost as if he knew she was hiding something.

'I haven't been here that long, and I like the area.'

'Over three years! What happened to your ambition?' He moved so close to her as he spoke that she couldn't escape his gimlet gaze.

'I'm in charge of this department.'

'You could run this with your beautiful blue eyes blindfolded.'

Panic at the increasingly personal nature of his comments made her rush into defending herself. 'I couldn't handle that interview at Rexford, so I reasoned that I needed more experience.'

'Tosh. I don't know what happened on the day of the interview, but you were the right candidate for that job and I hope you'll be as sorry as I am to learn that the person appointed in your stead has reduced the place to a shambles and is leaving.'

She flinched at his belligerent tone. He *hoped* she'd be sorry? Surely he didn't think she'd messed up the interview deliberately? Even now, the memory of that day haunted her dreams. The interview panel, all of whom she'd known so well, must have thought she'd done no preparation at all. 'I'm more than sorry to hear she's been a disaster, but I'm not surprised.'

He lifted a shoulder in an exaggerated shrug, but didn't speak.

She found his silent scrutiny worse than his probing questioning, and sought to escape it. 'Is that why *you* moved on?'

'Not totally, no. I got out before things were really bad, but I've kept in touch with the powers that be there and

I thought you might be interested to hear her job's up for grabs again.'

'Well, I'm not. Would *you* want to go back there?'

'Under the circumstances, probably not…'

She waited, but he didn't elaborate upon the circumstances he was referring to. When their eyes locked for long seconds she knew it wasn't about the department going down the pan.

To prove her uninterest, she checked her watch and muttered, 'I didn't realise it was lunchtime. I must check what the others are doing.'

'I'll see you down in the canteen,' he told her. 'Can I get you anything?'

'Er, no, I don't think so— I'm not sure if I'll get down immediately.' The last thing she wanted was a repeat of yesterday's débâcle.

'Right.' He gave her a long look. 'I suppose you're not free this evening, either?'

'No.'

'I thought not. See you later, then. You know where I am. Give me a shout if you *do* need me.'

He winked and sauntered out of her office, leaving her to wish the department was busier. If they were rushed off their feet she could probably cope—just—with them working together. But too much time for these conversational exchanges was dangerous.

Determined not to go down to the canteen while he was there, she sent a couple of her staff to lunch and took over the triage post for the next hour.

The first person to be directed to her by the receptionist was a mother with a toddler.

'He's hurt his head,' the mother announced as she walked into the room.

'Would you like to sit here with him on your knee?'

Once they were settled she smiled at the little boy and asked quietly. 'What have you done?'

He was clutching a dirty piece of blanket and, together with his thumb, inserted it into his mouth and turned away from Jenny.

''E fell down the stairs. Backwards. 'It his head on something and it's bleeding.' She pointed to a spot where the hair was matted with blood.

Jenny checked the card completed at Reception. 'He's nearly two, isn't he? Is he used to climbing stairs?'

'No—he was playing on the bottom two steps when it happened.'

'Did he hurt himself anywhere else?'

'I don't know. He hasn't said anything.'

'We'll get the doctor to look at the cut and she'll give him a once-over. Do you know what he hit his head on?'

'The floor, I suppose. Will it be long?'

Jenny pointed to the waiting time indicator. 'Probably no more than half an hour, unless we get an influx of serious cases. Is that a problem?'

The woman shrugged.

Jenny changed tack. 'Have you taken him for all his childhood injections?'

'He hasn't missed one,' she responded proudly.

'That should save some time. And you won't need to bring him back here if he needs stitches removed or a dressing changed. Your own doctor will do that for you.'

'That's the last place I'd take 'im.'

'Why's that?'

'It'd be months before 'e'd even see us—'

'Not if you explain when you make your appointment—'

'I'd rather come back here.'

Jenny frowned and shook her head. 'It's up to you, of course, but—'

'I'll come back here.'

Jenny nodded thoughtfully. 'OK. Now, if you'd like to take a seat over there, someone will see you when it's your turn.'

She went in search of Rosie. 'I've just seen a toddler, Kyle Smith, who has a cut on his scalp. Supposed to have happened when he fell down the bottom couple of stairs, but his mother is a bit vague about what happened. He looks well-nourished, but could you check him over for other injuries?'

'You think it might be non-accidental?'

'I don't really think so. Just being over-cautious. I told her you'd check him over as she wasn't sure if he'd hurt himself anywhere else. I think the cut might need a couple of sutures because of where it is.'

Rosie nodded. 'I'll see him next, and then hope to get some lunch.'

'If Annette's back I'll come down with you.'

Rosie was still busy with Kyle when Jenny was relieved from triage duties, so she caught up with some paperwork in the office while she waited.

Max found her there.

'Aren't you eating?'

'I'm waiting for Rosie. She's been checking out a toddler for me.'

'Problem?'

'Not now. Just me being over-cautious.'

'I had lunch with Andy.'

She nodded her approval.

'He's arranging a few drinks and nibbles after work tomorrow, so that I can meet the other consultants and departmental heads.'

'Good idea.'

'He asked me to tell you about it.'

'Right.'

'You'll be able to join us, will you?'

'Me? I don't need to be there, do I? You already know me.'

'I think he's expecting you. You ought to make the effort.'

'I'm busy tomorrow evening.'

'It'll only be for an hour or so.'

'I'll see what I can do.'

'You do seem to have a very full social life.'

He was pressing for answers again, and she didn't like it. 'For goodness' sake, Max, do you expect me to sit at home every evening, twiddling my thumbs?'

'Hey! Lighten up. You would have known in the old days that I was only teasing.' His voice held a trace of regret, but the heat of his gaze hinted at the intimacy they had once known.

Not needing the reminder, she averted her eyes and told him, 'Rosie and I are going to lunch. I'll tell Annette *you're* holding the fort.' She sped out of the office before he could argue.

They'd barely started eating their late lunch when Fran paged Jenny. 'Annette said could you both come as soon as possible? The police have brought in a man stabbed in a fight and his friends are continuing it in the waiting room.'

'I'll be right up. Get Security there immediately.'

When she saw the chaos that was now her department, Jenny's heart sank. She looked into the resus area and Annette indicated that the assembled trauma team were coping, watched over by two burly policemen.

'Anything you need?' she mouthed to Max.

He shook his head. 'By the sound of things you'd better get that lot sorted, before someone else gets hurt.'

A terrified Fran was cowering in a corner, as far away from the mêlée as possible, while two of the hospital's security men tried to separate and calm the two factions. 'Go in with Annette and let me know if they need anything.'

Fran scuttled away and Rosie joined Lisa, who had herded those from the waiting room who were not involved in the fight into the cubicles area and was trying to instil some order.

Jenny stationed herself by the main entrance to prevent anyone else entering the department unless it was a matter of life and death. Within minutes police reinforcements arrived, and one by one the combatants slunk away, only to find themselves detained by other police officers outside.

Jenny told any of the combatants who needed attention to remain in the waiting area and then, with the security men, started to right chairs and put the department back into some semblance of order.

'We have all their names and addresses. Do you want to press charges?' the senior policeman asked.

'I just want the place back to normal as soon as possible. Do you know what it was all about?'

'Drugs, I think. How's the original casualty?'

She nodded towards the resus room. 'In good hands. There's a couple of your men with him, too.'

'It was them called us to help you.'

'I'm glad they did, or goodness knows what would have happened.'

'Jack—' he indicated his colleague '—and I'll get some details from those other three waiting for your ministrations, and then we'll be off.'

Jenny nodded. 'I'm afraid they'll have a long wait.'

'Won't do them any harm,' he chuckled.

Relieved that it was all over as quickly as it had flared up, Jenny returned to the resus room to discover how the stab victim was faring.

Max looked up and shook his head ruefully, and she knew they'd lost the battle for their patient's life. He followed Jenny out of the room, stripping off his gloves and apron before he did so.

He slammed the office door behind them and, slumping in a chair, ground out, 'What a waste of a young life.'

Jenny knew how upset he was at losing the patient, and rested a hand on his shoulder in gesture of comfort. He leaned his cheek against it and took hold of her free hand.

'Thanks.' He kissed her palm. 'For being there.' He looked up and smiled, then pulled quickly away as the two original police officers joined them in the office.

'Sorry. I find failure difficult to come to terms with. Especially when it's a youngster.' Max shook his head.

'Will you be in touch with his relatives?'

'We're already looking, but no one seems to care about him,' the senior of the two police officers replied. 'Sad, but that's the way it often is these days. OK if we leave you to it now, Doc? We'll be in touch later.'

Max nodded, and when they'd gone Jenny said vehemently, 'He must have a mother somewhere. He's barely out of his teens.'

Max gave her a long hard look before saying, 'What about a father? Aren't you forgetting him? He must once have had one of those, surely?' He shrugged before adding bitterly, 'But maybe not. As the policeman said, who knows what way it is these days? What do you think, Jenny?'

Jenny tried hard to swallow the uncomfortable lump in

her throat and failed miserably. It was increasingly obvious that it was going to be difficult to continue working with Max. Perhaps it was her guilty conscience, but it seemed to her that every word he uttered had a double meaning—that he wasn't talking about the young lad who'd just died at all, but using the situation to try and make her open up to him. There was surely no way he could possibly know about Jamie. Was there?

Sudden panic gripped her at the thought that if he did know it would explain why he'd come to Catonbury. Clare was well again, but after chemotherapy would she be able to have a family? Her mind whirled. Perhaps he was hoping for a ready-made one? If so, it was even more important that he found out nothing about Jamie.

Fearful that he must at least be harbouring a suspicion that she was hiding *something*, Jenny sought to escape his relentless gaze. She pushed her chair back noisily and opened the office door. 'The waiting time must be building up alarmingly. I think we both ought to earn our keep.'

CHAPTER THREE

AWARE she was right, Max sighed and followed her out. But he was puzzled. He had taken this job for a couple of reasons. Certainly because it had become increasingly obvious that to get the top job he wanted he would need to show some out of London experience on his CV. And also because he knew Catonbury was a good hospital. But mainly because he'd been unable to forget Jenny Stalham.

But this was a very different Jenny from the open and friendly girl he had known three years ago. She was tetchy and evasive, and he wanted to know what or who had changed her. And why was she obviously keeping him at arm's length?

He knew it had been common knowledge at Rexford that he had taken compassionate leave because an old girl-friend was very ill, but one of the first things he'd done when he'd fallen in love with Jenny was to tell her about Clare, and how they'd known one another since childhood. He had thought she would understand his absence.

Sure now that it must be a form of madness that had led him to abandon his carefully worked out career plan for a woman he'd known for barely two months, he told himself he should have known better. Until he'd met Jenny he hadn't even intended to get married—well, not until he reached his ultimate goal of senior consultant—and he had thought she was quite happy with that, too, as she had her own career.

But she obviously hadn't been. He should have realised that when she'd taken off with another man. He had been every kind of a fool to waste even a moment yearning for her, let alone three years.

Hadn't she known where to find him all along? And what about this baby a locum colleague who had briefly worked at Catonbury had hinted at? Sure, Max had been shocked to hear that Jenny was a mother, but that hadn't stopped him wanting to see her again. Even if it was only to confirm once and for all that he had no place in her life. At least then he would finally be able to move on. But he hadn't heard any mention of a child so far, which was unusual for a proud mum. And neither was she wearing a wedding ring. Was she living with the father? If not, who was he? Someone they both knew? That would certainly explain why she was so edgy every time he spoke to her.

His reverie was shattered by someone tugging at his arm. Niall, a young doctor new to casualty work, who had joined the department a few days before, asked timidly, 'Can you take a look at this girl Melanie Cox for me? I can't make her out. She's barely thirty-five, her ECG is normal, but she's complaining of a chest pain typical of severe angina. Her pulse is pretty rapid.'

'Is she on the pill?'

He shook his head. 'Rosie suggested I check that. And there's no sign of deep vein thrombosis.'

'Is her temperature normal?'

'At the moment, yes, but she's sweaty. I think it's come down after the paracetamol she's taken for the pain.'

Max frowned. 'Chest X-rays?'

A deep flush stained Niall's cheeks. 'I didn't think them necessary at this stage. Her chest sounds normal.' At Max's surprised lift of an eyebrow, he tried to defend himself, 'We've had it drummed into us not to subject our patients to unnecessary X-rays.'

Max nodded thoughtfully. 'Sometimes it's the only way forward in cases like this. But not to worry. I'll take a look. See if I can spot something.'

Max read through the notes Niall had made, then followed him into the cubicle.

Jenny was talking to the girl, a voluptuous blonde who, on seeing Max, batted eyelashes heavily caked with mascara.

Niall stopped just inside the door, the flush creeping insidiously over his face. 'This is Mr Field. He'd like to take a look at you.'

'Can you show me exactly where this pain is, Melanie?'

'Sure.'

It was all Jenny could do not to laugh when Melanie brazenly bared her braless chest to show him.

He calmly resorted to his stethoscope to distance his initial examination of the exposed area. 'That all sounds fine,' he told her, then indicated to Jenny that she should cover her up. He moved round to the foot of the examination couch. 'I'd like to ask you a few more questions.'

He subjected the girl to what Jenny thought amounted to a cross-examination until he finally arrived at the answers he was looking for.

'What did you say you were drinking?'

'Cider.'

'Bottled?'

'No. Local stuff.'

'I suppose that's Catonbury's equivalent of Somerset scrumpy?' He looked to Jenny for confirmation but, not knowing anything about it, she shrugged.

'So. How much did you drink last night?' he asked.

'Six pints.'

Her answer was a long time coming, but when it did

Max lifted both his eyebrows and rolled his eyes towards Jenny and Niall before asking, 'And have you eaten anything today?'

'Black coffee—to take the tablets.'

'How much?'

'Four mugfuls, I think.'

Max wrote it all down and then said, 'Can you shuffle down the couch and let me examine your tummy.'

Jenny assisted Max to get access to her abdomen.

Several times when he asked her if it hurt, she nodded.

'Right. You can get dressed now.' His manner was brusque. 'I think your pain is more than likely due to inflammation of your stomach lining caused by the cider, the black coffee and lack of food. We'll get you an antacid preparation and keep you here for a little while to see if it works.'

He and Niall left the cubicle and Jenny followed almost immediately. They went into Jenny's office and Max closed the door behind them. He shook his head despairingly. 'When the pain improves refer her to her GP. And give the practice a ring rather than trust her with a letter.'

Jenny sorted through the notes and handed Niall Melanie's prescription sheet. 'If you write her up for the antacid I'll see to it—and try and educate her in the dangers of alcohol.'

'Ask the GP to do the same, would you, Niall? Or she'll be back in here again.'

The young doctor nodded, then asked, 'I suppose it was the coffee that caused the speeding pulse?'

'Or the after-affects of the alcohol. Probably a bit of both.' Max shrugged. 'Who knows what else she gets up to?'

Niall looked worried. 'I am sorry about dragging you into that…'

'Nothing to apologize for. She was enough to put anyone off their stroke. Experience counts for a lot in this
job.' Max patted Niall reassuringly on the shoulder and
grinned. 'You'll soon learn to recognise when you're not
being told everything. Won't he, Jenny?'

'I…er…guess so,' Jenny stuttered. Grabbing the prescription from Niall, she escaped from the office. Sure his
words again hid a double meaning, Jenny felt her earlier
sense of panic returning. She couldn't afford to allow Max
any closer. For Jamie's sake, that was something she must
never do.

Whatever had brought him here, once he'd completed
his contract at Catonbury he would move on, she was
sure. Probably back to London. So for the little lad's sake
Max must know nothing. It wouldn't be fair on Jamie for
him to get to know the father he hadn't realised existed
only to have him move on up the career ladder. It was far
better to leave things as they were.

Jenny had never known such a long afternoon. She
loved her work and the busier she was the better she usually enjoyed it. But not today. And this was only Max's
first day.

The moment she could hand over to Leanne she did so
and, eager to get home to her son, hastily prepared for her
escape. Max noticed and followed her to the changing
room door. 'Don't forget to plead for indulgence.'

Impatiently she swung round to face him. 'Wh-what—'

'The welcome get-together tomorrow. You hadn't forgotten, had you?'

She shook her head. 'Of course not.'

'You should only be an hour later than usual.'

'I know. I hadn't forgotten.' She was about to escape
when her curiosity about his private life got the better of
her. 'Haven't *you* a home you want to get back to?'

'I wouldn't exactly call it a home. I've found a flat for the moment, not far from here, but there are few home comforts to cause me to rush back there.'

Why, oh, why had she asked such a damn fool question? He was obviously angling for her sympathy but there was no way she could invite him to her house. Perhaps he wasn't married yet, or had decided not to move Clare up because he would be here for such a short time.

'I'll see you tomorrow, then.'

He nodded and walked away, but not before giving her another of his searching looks.

The more she thought about it the more her suspicions grew about his motives. It was obvious he was determined to find out more about her and she didn't like it. Not when she had Jamie to consider.

Her mother was only too pleased when Jenny mentioned the welcome party for the new consultant. Jenny had waited until Jamie was settled and they had eaten to broach the subject.

'Of course I don't mind you being late. You need to get out and meet people.'

'I'm doing that every day.'

'But not socially. Look at you. Only twenty-eight and a virtual recluse.'

'I don't have time.'

'You need to make it.'

Jenny grinned and tried to divert the conversation. 'What about you? When Jamie goes to school you'll be lost.'

'I keep in touch with my friends. They understand.'

Jenny nodded. 'So do mine.'

Her mother's answering smile was sceptical. 'You

don't need to rush home tomorrow, anyway. I'll put Jamie to bed.'

'I'll be back long before that.'

Her mother shook her head in despair and wandered through to her own quarters. Before going to bed herself, Jenny searched through her wardrobe for a suitable outfit to wear the next evening. Not wanting to wear anything that Max would remember, she eventually settled on jeans and a delicately embroidered cardigan top.

They were busy, but not hectically so, next morning. But it was enough to prevent Max tormenting her with his questions about her private life. Until she settled to her lunch.

Without asking, he took the seat opposite her and with a warm smile asked, 'How'm I doing?'

Surprised by his question, she told him, 'Fine. The morning went well, didn't it?'

'Were you granted permission to stay on this evening?'

She felt herself bristling at the phrasing of his question. 'I don't know what you mean.'

'Will you be at my welcome do?'

'I promised and I'll be there. But I don't need permission from anybody.'

'That's all right, then.' He sampled a forkful of his chicken curry and grimaced. 'It's not like yours used to be.'

'What do you expect? This is hospital food, after all.'

He nodded ruefully. 'I guess so. Perhaps if I behave you'll cook me one of your specials?'

She shrugged. 'Maybe. One day.' But don't hold your breath.

*   *   *

The drinks were already flowing freely when Jenny entered the hospital boardroom after changing out of her uniform. Andy rushed across to greet her. 'Jenny! How lovely to see you. What can I get you to drink?'

'A sparkling mineral water, please.'

'Coming up.' As he poured he called over his shoulder, 'Max. Look who's here.'

Jenny knew he didn't have to be told. Although he'd been chatting with an animated group of medics, his eyes had been drawn to her the moment she entered the room and they hadn't left her for a moment.

Andy handed her a glass and reluctantly she tore her own gaze away. 'Thanks for this. Look, don't disturb Max. I've been working with him all day.'

'He didn't expect you to turn up,' Andy blurted out. Then, trying to cover his confusion at divulging a confidence, rushed on to make matters even worse by saying, 'You don't usually come to these things, do you?'

'I thought I ought to welcome an old colleague.'

Andy nodded. 'I'm glad you made the effort. We were lucky to get him. A & E specialists can pick and choose where they work.'

Jenny frowned, and although she understood what he meant felt she had to make a token protest. 'What's wrong with our department here?'

'It's just that we're not in the right place. Nothing exactly wrong.'

'That's a relief.'

'I certainly wasn't criticising *your* work,' he hastened to reassure her. 'The place has improved immeasurably since you joined us.'

'So you agree with me it's time she went for promotion?' the deep voice she remembered so well enquired from behind her.

Jenny felt his hot breath brush her left ear and swung

round as if she'd been stung. 'You were eavesdropping,' she accused, hot colour flaming in her cheeks. 'Hoping to hear something good about yourself, were you?'

'Andy was talking about *you*. And I agree with every word he said.'

'How can you? You don't know what this department was like when I came here.'

'I don't know, no. But I've heard.'

'Do you mean internal promotion, Max? We don't want to lose Jenny. Certainly not just as we get a good consultant in post.'

'Would you please stop talking about me as if I'm not here?' she snapped. 'You're making me wish I hadn't made the effort to come.'

'Was it such a trial to spare me even a few moments of your free time?'

Max's intense scrutiny was making her uncomfortable, their exchange seemed to be having the same effect on Andy. When the boardroom door swung open he excused himself with obvious relief and rushed across to greet the latecomer.

She glared at Max. 'Stop looking at me like that. You've embarrassed poor Andy. Why don't you circulate? I thought this shindig was for you to meet the other consultants.'

He laughed. 'I'd hardly call such a respectable gathering a ''shindig''. And anyway, I met most of them earlier.'

'In that case I'm off home. You obviously don't need me to introduce you.'

'I need you to talk to me. Please?'

She checked her watch. 'Sorry, Max. I have to go.'

'You've only just arrived.'

'It's been a long day and I only said I'd show my face.'

'I'll see you to your car.' She sensed his exasperation with her.

'There's no need.'

She might as well have saved her breath. He waited until she had said her farewells to Andy, then followed her along the corridor. 'Eat with me, Jenny?'

'I'm sorry, I have to get home.'

He sighed. 'Pity. But thank you for "making the effort" to come.' He reached past her to open the main door, but changed his mind—and, before she realised his intention, lightly brushed her lips with his.

The flurry of sensation that his kiss aroused prevented her from moving for a moment, then she wrenched open the door without a word and sped out into the car park.

Max watched until she was safely in her car, then, ruefully shaking his head, turned to find Dan right behind him.

'Well, that was a first.'

'Um. What was?' Max was deep in thought about Jenny.

'I've never known Jenny Stalham attend a hospital event before. You must be pretty special to her.'

Max groaned, inwardly fuming because Dan had probably seen that kiss. Jenny wouldn't be at all amused if he started spreading rumours. 'She's an old friend and an excellent nurse.' He must somehow divert any suspicions Dan was harbouring.

'I'll admit she's that *and* a good-looker, but she's got a cold heart. She never accepts invitations out. I was told when I first came here not to get any ideas about her.'

'Perhaps she's already in a steady relationship? Or even married? Though I can't say there's any evidence of that.' Max seized the opportunity to discover if Dan knew more about her than he did.

'According to her file she's not married, but more and more couples prefer to live together these days. You'd think she'd bring him along to some of the hospital events, though.'

'Perhaps she has her reasons.'

'For being standoffish?' Dan's tone was bitter. 'Like what?'

'Well—an ailing boyfriend or parent who needs her attention, perhaps?'

Dan shrugged. 'If that's the reason, why doesn't she say so? Instead of giving the impression that none of us are good enough for her.'

Dan was clearly one of those Jenny had rejected, and he wasn't at all happy about it.

Max clapped him on the back. 'Don't take it personally, old chap. Her career is important to her and, as I said, she's an excellent nurse. And a good administrator. I've just been telling Andy she ought to be promoted. Come on—have a drink with me and forget her.'

It wasn't until some time later, when Max left the gathering for his temporary flat, that he had time to think about what Dan had said. Cold-hearted? That was the last description to fit the Jenny he had known at Rexford, and yet Dan wasn't the only one at Catonbury to describe her as a bit standoffish.

Max frowned as he thought things through. There certainly didn't seem to be any sign of a regular relationship. Perhaps she just didn't want to be involved with anyone— maybe with a child to think about, a relationship wasn't on the cards for her. That could be it. Unless—unless she *was* in a relationship, but it was with somebody she didn't want to be seen with at the hospital or talk about.

Surely she wasn't having an affair with a married man? One of the consultants he had been talking to that evening, perhaps? Was that why she had seemed so uncomfortable for the short time she was at the gathering?

He was puzzled. He didn't think she was the type to risk someone else's marriage. But then there was no accounting for love. He certainly couldn't. He had tried to forget her and move on, but the memory of what they had shared refused to go away.

Jenny's mind was in a whirl as she drove home. That brief kiss had reminded her just how much she loved him, despite the way he had cheated on her, and momentarily she was tempted to wonder if it was worth telling him about Jamie.

But common sense soon prevailed. For Jamie's sake, as well as her own, she knew that would spell disaster.

Max had made it perfectly clear from the start of their relationship that marriage and children didn't figure in his plans until he had completed all his exams.

When he'd first told her that she hadn't worried. She'd had her own career to concentrate on and there had been plenty of time.

And that was the reason she had fluffed the interview so badly. She'd loved him to distraction, and had been sure that if she'd told him she was pregnant he would offer to do the right thing and marry. her, but she hadn't wanted him to do that if it meant him not achieving his original ambition.

Because it had been all her fault. She had reassured him she was on the pill, forgetting in the heat of their passion the tummy bug she had suffered early in her cycle. So when, the night before he'd set off for his study leave, their lovemaking had proceeded to its inevitable climax and they hadn't used protection.

At first, Jenny had kept telling herself she would be

more likely to win the lottery than to get pregnant. But her numbers hadn't come up and her breakfast had. For the three days leading up to the interview. So she hadn't got the job.

She would never, ever regret Jamie's birth, though. If she couldn't have Max, Jamie was the next best thing, and he had certainly brought her closer to her mother.

Although she'd known Max didn't intend to start a family so soon, if he'd contacted her she would have told him. But not now. It had been too late the moment she'd discovered Clare was more than the platonic friend he'd said she was.

It still hurt to discover that she had never meant anything to him more than someone to pass the time with at Rexford. Clare was welcome to him.

The moment she had taken the hand-over report next morning Max stormed into her office, banging the door back against the wall as he came through.

Rarely having seen him in such a strop, she remonstrated, 'Max! What on earth's the matter?'

He closed the door more quietly behind him. 'Have you spoken to that paramedic yet?'

'Patrick. Um—no. I haven't had a chance.'

'Well, if you don't do it today, I will.'

'Why? What—?'

'He brought in a girl who'd taken an overdose earlier, and told her mother the girl would be better off dead.'

'Better off—?' Jenny frowned. 'Did he say why?'

'I don't believe this. Does it matter?' Max snapped. 'He's no right saying things like that.'

'I guess not. Is—is he still out there?'

'He's gone to the canteen for breakfast, leaving us to pick up the pieces.'

'Where is the mother?'

'Having a coffee in the relatives' room. I'm on my way back there.'

'I'll go down and see Patrick.'

'You do that. Because I'm not prepared to put up with him upsetting anybody else. I'm tempted to put in a formal complaint as it is.'

'Let me talk to him before you do that. Please, Max?'

He strode from the office without comment.

When she joined Patrick at a table in the corner of the dining room, he was staring into space, his breakfast uneaten and a bottle of tablets in front of him.

She smiled. 'Hello, Patrick. Can I join you?'

He looked up and started to nod, then stilled his head with his hands.

'Aren't you feeling very well?'

He didn't say anything immediately and then muttered, 'Headache.'

'Have you taken some paracetamol?'

'Doc gave me these. He said they were stronger.' He handed her the pot on the table.

'Your GP?'

He nodded.

She checked the date on the bottle. 'You've had them for a while?'

'Aye.'

'Did he say what the headache was? You don't look as if you should be at work to me.'

'A virus.'

She frowned. 'A virus doesn't usually take this long to clear. Why don't you come up and let one of our docs take a look at you?'

He looked at his watch. 'I must get back to Mike. He stayed in the ambulance.' He stood up, and with a groan immediately sat down again. 'It's not been this bad before.'

'You can't drive like this. I'll find Mike.'

Jenny took his arm and they walked slowly to the lift.

She persuaded him to lie down in an empty cubicle and, after warning Annette he was there, went in search of Max.

He was looking at an X-ray of a leg.

'I saw Patrick.'

'The fibula's cracked—there.' He pointed at the small bone in the lower leg.

'Max, I saw Patrick and I think he's ill.'

'Tell him to see his GP.'

'He's already seen him.'

'What was the verdict?'

'Virus. But I think it's something more serious.'

Max took the X-ray from the machine and attached it to the patient's notes. 'In what way?'

'I don't know, but I have a vague memory at the back of my mind about a patient at Rexford who'd undergone a personality change. It turned out to be a brain tumour.'

'I thought you said he had wife trouble.'

'I didn't say… Max.' She touched his arm. 'Would you just take a quick look at him to set my mind at rest?'

He sighed. 'If I must. Then I need to do something about this broken leg.'

'I'll come along with you, and then I must go and tell Patrick's colleague where he is.'

Mike seemed relieved to hear that someone was taking a look at Patrick. 'He's been impossible since he's had these headaches.'

'How long's he been like this?'

'He hasn't been right for some time, but these last couple of weeks…' He shrugged, clearly unwilling to shop a colleague.

Max met them at the door. 'I'm afraid your mate's not fit to work this morning. Who should I contact?'

'I'll give base a call. Will he be OK tomorrow?'

'I'll let them know.'

'You think it's a virus as well?'

'Maybe. I'm going to run a few tests.'

Jenny walked back to the office with Max. 'Well?'

'I've organised a CT scan. Leanne's taken him down.'

'You think—?'

'I'll tell you later. I'm going to see that broken leg.'

'Shouldn't Rosie be dealing with it?'

He tapped his nose with a forefinger. 'It's one of the radiographers. How do you think I managed to get the scan so easily.'

Jenny shook her head in mock despair and went in search of Annette to see what needed doing next.

It was much later in the morning before she saw Max again.

'You know Patrick's wife, don't you?'

She nodded. 'Why?'

'Will she be at work?'

'I think I can contact her, if that's what you're asking. Was it—?'

'I've asked the neuro team to take a look at him. I think he'd like her there.'

She lifted the receiver. 'Now?'

He nodded. 'I spoke to the registrar. They'll be down when they've finished in the clinic.'

'Leave it with me. What do I tell her?'

'The truth. Say you were worried about the headaches and asked someone to take a look at him.'

She rang the florist where Sarah worked and relayed

her message. It was some time before she could replace the receiver. 'She's on her way. She's so grateful that somebody is doing something. Says he's been difficult for weeks. Mike said the same.'

Max slotted a film into the viewing cabinet. 'And that's why, I imagine.' He pointed to a small lesion at the front of the brain. He walked round to her side of the desk and, grasping her shoulders, repeated the light kiss of the previous evening. 'Thank you, Sister Stalham.'

The faint aroma of his aftershave mingled with the familiar taste of him surprised her and left her aching for more. She pulled back from him sharply and, when she could trust her voice not to waver, asked, 'What for?'

'The spot-on diagnosis. And caring about the man.' As he spoke his eyes searched her face, as if expecting a reaction. 'I was much less forgiving.'

'You didn't—don't really know him. And it wasn't until *you* pointed out how he was upsetting people that *I* took notice of the change in his personality.'

'As I believe I've said before, we're a good team.'

He was still standing too close for her comfort and she needed to escape. 'Have you had coffee?'

He sighed deeply. 'I have, but if that's all that's on offer I suppose I can always down another.'

Ignoring his pointed hint, she said, 'I'll prime the machine and then check the state of play. Sarah is probably here already.'

Sarah was just coming through the main doors of the department. She saw Jenny and rushed across. 'Where is he? What's happening?'

'Come into the office for a minute and meet our new consultant.'

'You're Patrick's wife?' Max greeted her with an outstretched hand. 'Glad you could come. He isn't at all well this morning, so Jenny asked me to take a look at him. His head is obviously troubling him and I've asked one of my colleagues up.'

'You think it's something serious?'

'Sarah…' he said gently. 'May I call you Sarah?'

When she nodded he poured her a cup of coffee, then went on. 'Jenny tells me she's noticed a change in your husband recently, but as I've only just met him I'd rather wait and see what the expert has to say.'

'He's different, all right. Everything I do is wrong. I thought it was me, then I realised nothing I did would suit him. I thought he wanted out of our marriage—that he must have another woman—it's been awful—the kids have noticed it, too.'

Relief at being able to pour out her fears to sympathetic listeners loosed her tongue in a way that was clearly new to Sarah, and they didn't try to stop her. Max made a few notes about Patrick's bizarre behaviour at home, and when the torrent eventually began to dry up he suggested Jenny took Sarah to wash her face and then to see her husband.

When she returned he was still writing. 'OK?'

'He's asleep. She's stayed with him. Holding his hand.'

'She's worried. Even so, it must be a relief to discover there's a reason for his behaviour.'

Jenny nodded thoughtfully, suddenly overwhelmed by the thought of what it would be like if it they were a family unit and it was Max who was ill. She shuddered, and turned to pour herself a coffee before he noticed her agitation.

He didn't look up. 'She certainly needed to get all that off her chest. I've written up lot of what she said in his notes. I don't think she'll give such a detailed history to anyone else.'

'I guess not. Help yourself to coffee.' She had to get

away. Immediately. Before she did something she would regret. 'I think I'm needed to cope with some of the waiting hordes. I'll let you know when the neuro men appear.'

'I'll just finish this and join you.' He glanced up and frowned. 'Hey! Stop worrying over things you can't do anything about. Patrick's in good hands.'

He moved towards her as he spoke and she pulled open the door. 'I know—I must go. Rosie's coping with a couple of suspected heart attacks in resus.'

'I'll take a look in a minute. Are there any beds?'

'Not on CCU. That's for sure.'

'I'll give Andy a ring. He can do some work for his living.'

It was like bedlam in the waiting area. The waiting time indicator was up to three hours and there wasn't a cubicle empty. Jenny and Max worked right through the lunch break to try and get the numbers down.

The neuro team came briefly, agreed it was probably a tumour of sorts and admitted Patrick. Beyond that they wouldn't commit themselves.

It was nearly three before Jenny escaped to her office again and refreshed the coffee machine.

Max joined her a few moments later. 'What did we do to deserve that?'

'Recompense for the quiet morning yesterday?'

He nodded ruefully. 'I guess so. But I'd rather have them evened out.'

'Wouldn't we all? I'm starving.'

'Me, too. We deserve a treat tonight to make up for it. Join me?'

She was immediately serious. 'I'm sorry, Max. I can't.'

'I'm only suggesting a meal so that we can talk. There's never enough time here.'

'I know, but—'

'I was impressed with your diagnosis of Patrick. You know, you could do so much better for yourself. Why stay here?'

'I have my reasons.'

He studied her for a long moment, his gaze causing her to dread what he'd say next. 'The same reasons that made you cut and run from Rexford?'

She swallowed hard. 'No—not really. I've told you why I did that. The interview—'

He clearly dismissed that answer as unworthy of comment. 'I thought it might be the same reason that ensures you are never able to accept an invitation because you don't have a free evening?'

Flustered, she shrugged, but didn't speak in case her voice let her down. Why wouldn't he leave her alone?

'Do you have other commitments, Jenny?' His thundering voice broke in on her thoughts. She felt the colour draining from her face. He must know something!

'Commitments? Like what?'

'Looking after your child, for instance?'

CHAPTER FOUR

SHE'D started to rise from her chair, but his words made her sink back again, her face frozen. 'What are you talking about?'

'That locum who worked here for a while—he was a mine of information.' All the time he was speaking his eyes were searching her face, as if to discover the truth. 'He told me you weren't married, but he had an idea you had a child.'

'How could he? No one knows—' She broke off, realising she had just told him what he wanted to know.

'The locum was Peter Wentworth. Remember him?'

'I—er—think so.' And she'd been so sure he hadn't guessed.

'I thought you might. He overheard you taking a call when Jamie was ill, didn't he? You tried to convince him it was a nephew, but when you left work almost immediately he worked out it was *your* child. It was lucky for you he was moving on the next day or your secret would have been out.'

When she didn't speak he grasped her left hand in his. 'So. Why no wedding ring?'

'It's not a crime in this day and age—if it ever was,' she snapped heatedly.

'I didn't say it was. How old is he?'

'My son? Nearly two.' Behind her back, Jenny crossed her fingers. She hated telling him a lie, but it was necessary. Not only for Jamie, but for Max, as well as herself.

'So the father is someone you met here?'

'Does it matter?'

'Or was he the reason you left Rexford?'

She couldn't believe the way all her lies were boomeranging in one spot. 'I didn't—' She stopped, afraid of what she might let slip out next. His piercing gaze coupled with his probing for the truth was muddling her, especially when he twisted everything she had said. 'Maybe—yes.'

'Maybe?' He frowned. 'What kind of an answer is that? Either he was or he wasn't?'

'All right, if you have to know. He was. Happy?'

'Not happy, no.' Could he ever be happy again, knowing that she had transferred her affections so readily? She certainly couldn't have felt about him the way he did about her. 'But at least I know the truth now. Is he still around? Living with you? I take it from your earlier comments that you're not married.'

Jenny inclined her head. 'I don't think any of this—'

'Is my business? That's what you're about to say, isn't it? Well, I'm sorry, Jenny. I thought we had something going for us back there at Rexford, but I was obviously wrong.'

'I—I don't believe I'm hearing this,' she spluttered. 'You thought—?' She gasped. 'You dare to accuse me, when all the time you had a girlfriend waiting at home? You were using me to pass the time at Rexford. Nothing more.'

She tried to pull away as he grasped both her hands in his. 'Jenny—Clare was—is—a friend. And a girl. Nothing more. I told you about her when we first met.'

'And I believed you.'

'It was the truth.'

'Huh—so why the compassionate leave?'

'I've known her for a long time, Jenny. Our families were—are—close friends and neighbours, so we grew up together. In fact, she was the sister I didn't have. I took the time off as much for her parents—and mine—as for her.'

'You expect me to believe that?'

He shrugged. 'Whatever. It's too late now. You have a family, and the last thing I want to do is jeopardise your happiness.'

'I'm glad to hear that, at least.' She was instantly contrite as she remembered her suspicions about his intentions. Although she still wasn't sure she could believe him about Clare. His mother certainly hadn't.

'When you came here I thought *you* were probably already married to Clare.'

He shook his head in disbelief. 'I shouldn't have come. As soon as I can I'll get out of your life.'

Perversely, after the way she'd been feeling about his presence, she didn't want to lose him again so quickly. 'But your contract—'

'I'll speak to Andy as soon as possible. But obviously I can't leave immediately. In the meantime we'll just have to work together.'

He flung open the door, leaving her to regret what she had said. Why hadn't she denied everything, or at least made up a more plausible story? He looked so hurt, so desolate—and no wonder when she had deliberately led him to believe she had been two-timing him. For a moment she was tempted to call him back and tell him the truth.

But common sense prevailed and she stayed where she was, even though it was hard. If only he hadn't reappeared in her life she might eventually have forgotten him, but he had, and her memory of their time together was painful.

As Jamie's memories would be if he learnt that Max

was his father and then lost him again almost immediately because a better job offer turned up.

No. If it meant a sacrifice on Jenny's part then that was the way it had to be. She'd survived for the past four years and she would continue to survive.

Max immersed himself in the work of the department for the remainder of the afternoon. He didn't want to think about what Jenny had told him. Work was preferable. Immediately he'd left her he'd tried to contact Andy, but discovered he was at a meeting and wouldn't be back. Probably just as well. It would allow him to get his thoughts in order first.

Rosie must have noticed his mind wasn't completely on his work.

'Is there anything wrong, Max?'

'No. Why should there be?'

'Just you don't look your usual sunny self.'

He knew she was genuinely concerned, but he didn't feel like talking to anybody until he had had a chance to come to terms with the knowledge that his move to Catonbury had been a complete waste of time and effort.

'Probably tired.'

She nodded. 'I know the feeling. Would you like to join me for a meal?'

He was about to refuse when his memory of recent events made him hesitate. Now he knew that Jenny was out of reach, the sooner he got her out of his system the better. There was no way he would do anything to jeopardise her family. He'd always believed that children and their fathers need one another, and if the guy was still on the scene he had no option but to bow out gracefully.

He liked Rosie, she was a damned good doctor, and

perhaps, now he knew where he stood, she might be the right person to help him forget.

'That's good of you, Rosie. But not tonight. How about tomorrow evening?'

She gave him a wide grin. 'That'd be fine. Give me more chance to prepare the food. And clear up the flat.'

'Hey, I don't expect you to go to all that trouble. We'll go out. Tell me which is the best place to eat hereabouts and I'll book a table.'

'I enjoy cooking, so you're very welcome. Unless you feel you might be compromised, coming to my humble abode?'

'Perish the thought. I'll look forward to it.'

Max worked late and collected a takeaway Indian meal on the way back to his flat. By the end of the evening he had more or less worked out what he needed to say to Andy the next morning, and how he was going to cope with working alongside Jenny until such time as he could move on.

They had always worked together well, and there was no reason why they couldn't go on doing that. But as friends. Nothing more. It was no doubt his determination to find out the truth that had made her so tetchy since his arrival. So no more prying and upsetting her. He had all the answers he needed. Jenny was not available. If he now stopped pressuring her she would relax and he would see again the girl he had known and loved.

The only thing that worried him was the meal the following evening with Rosie. It had seemed such a lifeline when she'd offered, but he realised now he would be using her, and that wasn't fair. She was too nice a person to be hurt in that way. He would tell her so at the first opportunity.

He didn't get any better a night's sleep than he'd had

since he'd embarked on this foolhardy course of action. Despite what he now knew, thoughts of Jenny again invaded his thoughts, and when he did eventually drop off, she filled his dreams.

Rosie was nowhere to be seen when he arrived on duty, and he was told by the secretary that he couldn't have an appointment with Andy until late morning. All he could do was get stuck into work. And there was plenty of that.

'Another lorry pile-up on the motorway,' Jenny told him only twenty minutes later. 'The third in as many weeks. Three casualties at least in this one, though by the sound of it there's nothing can be done for one of them.' She shuddered. 'I lose sleep imagining how it must be for families expecting their loved one home from work as usual and being confronted with the news.'

The anguish in her face made him want to take her in his arms and comfort her, but he recognised it was no longer his place. All he could do was offer her a platitude.

'It doesn't bear thinking about, does it? All we can do is our best for those pulled out alive.' He turned abruptly on his heels and headed for the resus room. 'I'll check everything's ready.'

His curt response sent Jenny's heart plummeting. She should have obeyed her instinct and gone to him last night and confessed. Despite the impossibility of the situation, she still loved and cared about him. So much so that she couldn't bear him thinking badly of her. She hadn't set out deliberately to hurt him. Quite the opposite. Everything she had done she had thought was for the best, but now it seemed all she had succeeded in doing was making not only Max unhappy, but herself as well.

And what about Jamie? At the moment he was secure in the love of an all-female household, which was all he'd ever known. But was that wrong? Despite the disruption to his young life it might cause, would it be better for him to know his father? Even if there was a likelihood that he wouldn't stay around?

Despite the mounds of advice available on child rearing, she didn't believe she had ever heard anyone say definitively which of these two options was best for a child. She sat down at her desk with her head in her hands. She'd made a hopeless mess of things.

The sound of ambulance sirens jerked her into action. 'I'll assist you in resus,' she told Annette, 'and Lisa can take charge out here.'

The first casualty was rushed through on a trolley and met by Max, who nodded to Annette and Jenny to assist. 'We'll need everyone to move him across on my count. One... Two... Three.'

'He was thrown from the cab of his lorry. He's been unconscious since we attended. Blood pressure's falling rapidly. I think there must be massive internal bleeding, not to mention that head injury. We got one line in.'

'Do we know his name?'

'He has papers in the name Grey. Richard Grey.' The paramedic thumbed further through them and said, 'Looks like he's known as Rickie.'

'Richard? Rickie? Can you hear me?' Max got no response to either name, so he started to carry out a thorough examination while Annette and Jenny gently undressed Richard and attached monitor leads.

Another trolley was wheeled through, but the car driver on it was conscious. 'We can probably slide this chap across,' the paramedic told them. 'Main problem seems to be the leg injury. And shock.'

Rosie had joined Max as he was completing his examination of the first casualty. 'Take a quick look at that man and I'll give you a shout if I need you back here. You help Rosie, Annette. Jenny stay and help me.'

A few moments later Rickie's heart stopped beating. Max and Jenny worked tirelessly for the next forty minutes to try and restart it, but without success.

Max looked across at Jenny and shook his head. 'I think we should stop. His injuries are too extensive. You agree?'

Jenny continued what she was doing as if she hadn't heard.

'What about you, Rosie?' She had joined them in their efforts. 'I know Jenny of old. She hates to accept defeat.'

Rosie nodded. 'You're right. We've done all we possibly could.' She noted the time of death in his notes.

Jenny looked from one to the other, then gently covered Rickie, tears glinting in her eyes.

Max put an arm around her shoulder. 'Come away. You're exhausted.'

'We need to make him tidy for his mother to see. She's already on her way here.'

'All in good time. Get yourself a coffee and I'll help Rosie and Annette sort the car driver out.'

She shook her head and moved away from his light hold which was having an unbelievable effect on her body. 'I'm OK, thanks.'

'I guess it's not as easy to distance yourself when you're a mother yourself.'

She couldn't decide from his smile whether he was sympathising or seizing another opportunity to find out more about her child. 'I just hate the needless waste of a young life.'

'You're not alone in that, love. And, please don't ever stop being the caring person you are.' His eyes met hers and she read a warmth there that sent her senses reeling.

Unable to drag her gaze away, she felt her body tense in response.

He was the first to move, and she remained motionless as she watched him reluctantly make his way in to see the other casualty. His earlier brusqueness had hurt, but his use of the endearment while her emotions were so vulnerable had twisted her heart painfully.

He must still care about her if he had come looking for her—albeit four years later. She'd thought he must have forgotten all about her. Perhaps she had been wrong all along. Maybe they could have worked something out if he'd known about the pregnancy from the beginning.

The arrival of the orthopaedic team to assess the car driver's injury was a welcome diversion from her churning thoughts. They agreed to admit and treat him immediately as they had one empty bed. Once all the arrangements were made, and Leanne had gone with him to the ward, Jenny slipped into her office to grab the coffee Max had suggested earlier.

She wondered if he would join her, but only Rosie appeared. 'Max said he had an appointment with Andy.'

Any hope Jenny was secretly harbouring that Max might have changed his mind about leaving immediately was dashed. So it was decision time. Should she ask him to meet her that evening and tell him about his son, stressing she wasn't trying to trap him but felt he ought to know? Or should she keep quiet, as she had originally intended?

The truth was suddenly so blindingly clear that she couldn't believe she hadn't done something about it before. Jamie was his son and she was sure Max would never do anything to hurt him if he could help it. Max ought to know—and as soon as possible. Whatever it did to the way he felt about her.

* * *

While Max had been in Andy's office, Jenny had been coping with a fractious child who'd hurt his arm. She was now telling his mother she didn't think an X-ray was necessary, then Max stuck his head round the cubicle curtain.

'Need any help?'

She shot him an apprehensive glance before saying, 'No—well—er—yes. You could take a look at this wrist for me.'

At that moment nothing was so important to Jenny as knowing what the outcome of his meeting with Andy was, but she knew the welfare of her young patient came first.

Max gave no indication of what had happened, but turned to the little boy and his mother and asked how the injury had occurred.

The sonorous timbre of his voice appeared to quieten the child, and Jenny flashed him a brief smile of thanks.

She had already told the mother that she was sure there was no injury to the bones, and to her relief he confirmed this. 'I don't think there is any need to subject him to an X-ray. I think he just needs to rest it. If you're at all worried, bring him back or take him to see your GP.'

The moment the mother and child had gone, she asked, 'Everything OK, Max?'

'Sure. Shouldn't it be?'

She flushed at him making it so clear that after her rejection of him it was none of her business. To hide her discomfort she walked off and called the next patient on the list through to the treatment area that was now empty.

A little later her misery was compounded when she saw him in deep conversation. It was Rosie he'd told he was going to see Andy, not her, and now he was clearly sharing with her what had transpired at the meeting. It hurt. Especially as she knew it was her own fault.

She threw herself into her work and tried to tell herself that it didn't mean Rosie meant anything to him, he just needed someone to talk to and it could no longer be her.

It was soon clear how wrong she was.

An excited Rosie confided in her, probably because of what Jenny had said about him on his first day. 'Max seems so much more knowledgeable than that last consultant we had. He seems to know about even the most obscure conditions.'

'I think the comparison is a bit unfair, Rosie,' Jenny told her shortly. 'Mr Johnson was not a physician, but a surgeon. A totally different speciality.'

'Maybe, but my vote goes for Max. I've offered to make him a meal tonight. Can't be much fun being in a flat here on his own.'

Jenny stared at Rosie, her heart pumping painfully. She was too late. She'd made it clear to him that she wasn't interested and so he'd set out to find someone who was. Just when she'd decided she should involve him in her life again. He would think it petty jealousy if she told him the truth now.

It was Max's first weekend in Catonbury and he was working all day Saturday. Surprisingly the department was quiet during the day, which allowed him time—perhaps more than he really wanted—to think about his future.

He'd agreed with Andy to remain at the hospital until the end of his contract, but it would certainly be no longer—which didn't give him enough time to buy a property in the area, or even make it worthwhile moving his furniture down from his house at Rexford. But he couldn't decide whether to remain in the unprepossessing flat he was in at present, or look around for something better to rent.

He eventually decided he would allow chance to settle it. He had Monday off, so would remain in Catonbury and see what else the area had to offer. If he found something that really appealed to him he would go for it, otherwise he would forget the idea. It wasn't really important, because usually he would be returning to his Rexford home whenever he had time off.

The problem of Jenny wasn't as easy to settle. Working in such close proximity to her was doing nothing to help him forget what she'd meant to him. Rosie had cooked him a superb meal, and he'd enjoyed being with her. But his respect for her was such that he'd felt it only fair to explain why he wasn't ready for a relationship.

Without mentioning Jenny by name, of course. He'd also told Rosie that he would be moving on sooner rather than later.

She'd been very understanding. 'I'll be moving on as well. So why don't we just enjoy ourselves for now and take it as it comes?'

He'd still felt he was using her, and she didn't deserve that, but when he'd said as much, she'd grinned and said, 'We'll be using one another. I don't intend settling down until I finish my exams. Relationships are a distraction. This way we can both have company when we feel like it and not feel guilty when we don't.'

Monday afternoon turned out sunny, after a morning's rain, so he strolled down the High Street to look in the windows of the large number of letting agents there. He found nothing remotely of interest, so after purchasing some fresh fruit from the greengrocers he decided he would walk back to the hospital through the park. He could spend the rest of the afternoon catching up on some reading in the hospital library.

As he passed the playground area a young child came running at full pelt towards him, not watching where he was going but calling over his shoulder, 'C'mon, Granny. You run, too.'

'Watch—' Max tried to stop him falling over a broken branch lying on the ground, but he was too late. The boy tripped and sprawled chin down at Max's feet.

He picked him up and set him on his feet as his panicking grandmother caught up with him. 'Oh, Jamie. What on earth've you done now?'

Max, who was examining the graze, said reassuringly, 'The only damage seems to be to his chin, and if you just wash it well there should be no problem. As long as he had all his injections as a baby.'

'He'll be fine, thanks.' Despite her smile of gratitude, she moved the boy to her side and out of his reach. Recognising it was an instinctive wariness of strangers, he replaced his sunglasses, smiled, and set off in the direction of the hospital. But not before he'd taken a second look at her face. It was so familiar. He could have sworn he'd met her before, but she had shown no sign of recognition. It must have been in the A & E department, either as a patient or a relative of a patient.

Thankful that at least she hadn't expected him to remember why she had been to the hospital, he promptly forgot all about them both.

It had been a long day. Busy at times, but not busy enough to keep Jenny's mind occupied. It was Max's day off and she missed him being around. Even more than she had when she'd made the break four years ago.

She tried to tell herself it was his calming efficiency in

the department that she missed, but in reality she knew it was much more than that. He was Jamie's father, and if the timing had been better she and Max would probably have married and brought their son up together.

The trouble was she no longer believed she had made the right decision when she'd found herself pregnant. She realised she hadn't given him a chance to explain about Clare, and now here he was with a son he knew nothing about whilst dating Rosie.

It's too late for regrets, she told herself firmly as she drove home that evening. Jamie was the most important person in her life and she must concentrate on him. He was a settled and happy child, and she was determined he would stay that way, no matter what happened with Max.

As Jamie raced to the door to greet her he pointed to his chin and said, 'I did that baddie in the park.'

Jenny swept him up into her arms. 'You did what?'

'I—I fell over, an-and—' he stuttered with excitement as he tried to tell her everything at once 'I—I—I hurt my chin.' His lower lip wobbled as he sensed an opportunity for sympathy.

'Let me look.' She set him down and, turning his face towards the window, examined the graze.

'It's nothing much,' she reassured him. 'I'll kiss it better.'

Happy again, he ran off shouting, 'Mummy kissed my chin better.'

Her mother appeared with an apologetic smile.

'He was in too much of a hurry, as usual, and not looking where he was going. I've washed it well.'

Jenny nodded. 'Don't worry about it. He'll be fine.'

'That's what Granny told the man,' Jamie informed her seriously.

'Man? What man?'

'He picked me up.'

Jenny gave her mother a questioning look.

'He was walking towards us when Jamie fell and got to him before me. The way he checked there was no serious damage and asked about his childhood injections I guess he was probably a doctor. Especially as he was walking in the direction of the hospital.'

Too busy concentrating on what Jamie was telling her about the rest of his day, Jenny answered absently, 'That was good of him.'

Later in the evening, once Jamie was settled, she told her mother. 'I'm thinking about taking some time off, I feel I need a complete change, and I want to spend a bit of time with Jamie.'

'Good idea. You have been looking peaky recently. Where shall we go?'

'I haven't decided yet.' She smiled at her mother. 'I wasn't sure if you'd want to come with us or if you'd prefer to spend time with some of your friends. You deserve a rest and a change as well.'

'If you want me, I'd much prefer to come with you. However well-meaning, I always find staying with friends more exhausting than being with Jamie!'

'Of course we want you.' Jenny laughed as she hugged her. 'But I didn't want to take you for granted any more than I do already. I don't deserve you. You choose where we go.'

'Home or abroad?'

'Abroad is probably cheaper, but not too hot. For Jamie's sake.'

'Somewhere like Majorca?'

'Sounds great.'

'I'll get some brochures tomorrow.'

Jenny was glad she had the thought of a holiday to keep

her going the next day. Max was back after his day off and it seemed that every time she needed to speak to either him or Rosie they were chatting together. And not always about the patients.

The house officer made no secret of her admiration for Max and he was enjoying every minute of it. And why not? She was a doctor—a good doctor, Jenny had to admit. And a good friend. So if she was going to lose him at least it was to someone she liked.

She didn't have a chance to talk to Max face to face until mid-afternoon when, after a succession of trauma cases, he joined her in her office. 'Any chance of tea?'

'You must have smelt it.' Jenny filled one of the multicoloured mugs and handed it to him with a smile.

Max took the mug gratefully and, after swallowing a mouthful said, 'That's like nec…' He never completed the comparison because his voice tailed off as he looked at her properly for the first time that day.

'Something the matter, Max?' she asked.

He hurriedly pulled himself together and tried to drag his gaze away from her face. It was just a trick of the light. It must be. But for a moment he'd thought he was looking at a younger version of the grandmother of the young lad who had fallen at his feet the day before. Now he knew why he had been so sure he had met the woman before. He just couldn't believe he hadn't recognised it immediately.

CHAPTER FIVE

'IT WAS just…' He stopped, searching for an explanation.

'Ye-es?' she prompted.

'How old did you say your son is?'

'My son?' she queried, a look of amazement on her face. 'Nearly two. Why do you want to know?'

Aware that the boy who'd grazed his chin must have been at least three, he grimaced. 'No reason. I must have made a mistake.'

'What about?'

'Nothing important, really. It was…'

'Was what?' she demanded impatiently.

'Does he go to a crèche while you're at work?'

She frowned. 'Nursery school. Some days. Is that a problem?'

'No problem at all. I was just intrigued to know how you manage so well. Not many people here know you have a child, do they?'

'I prefer to keep it that way.'

He nodded thoughtfully, wanting to ask the reason for that and deciding he couldn't. However much he'd love to know, it really was none of his business who the child's father was. He changed the subject completely.

'Have you heard how that paramedic with the brain tumour is getting on?'

'Patrick?'

He nodded.

'They're operating this afternoon. I saw Sarah at lunch-

76

time. He'd just gone down to Theatre and she came to the canteen for a coffee. I said I'd go up and see them later.'

Andy Moss joined them before he could reply. 'Max. That stabbing last week?'

'What about it?'

'One of his mates has accused you of not doing enough, to save him.'

'Nothing could be further from the truth, could it, Jenny?'

'You don't have to convince me. But I thought I ought to warn you.'

'Thanks, Andy. So what now?'

'As he's written a letter of complaint there'll have to be a hospital enquiry.'

'What a waste of public time and money.'

'I'm inclined to agree with you. Gone are the days of letters of gratitude for what's been done in difficult circumstances.'

'That's because they come directly to us.' Jenny smiled. 'That board is full of thank-you cards. Look. Not everyone complains.'

Andy returned her smile. 'You're always a tonic, Jenny. That's the only reason I come here in person and don't telephone.'

'Only if you know we aren't desperate to find beds. Isn't that right, Andy?' Max teased. 'And I think we getting very near that stage now.'

Andy laughed and sped out of the department before they could make any demands.

'We'd better return to the fray as well. Then I might get away on time for once.'

An hour and half later Jenny checked her watch and, discovering she was already late off duty, raced across to

ITU. Sarah was seated in the visitors' room, staring blindly at a blank wall. When she turned, Jenny enveloped her in a hug.

'What's the news?'

'They seem pleased with the way the operation went, and say the tumour was successfully removed—all of it. But...' She closed her eyes for a brief second. 'They won't guarantee he'll be back to what he was.'

'I don't expect they will. Until he's fully conscious and they've tested his responses there's no way they can know what damage the tumour may have done. But it sounds as if they're pretty optimistic. Have you seen him?'

Sarah sighed. 'He's still flat out. The nurse suggested I go home, but...' She sniffed. 'I'd rather stay. In case he wants me.'

'I should go and have a meal, at least. You won't be any use to him if you're fading away with hunger.'

Sarah rubbed her forehead, her exhaustion obvious. 'You're probably right, but I won't go until they've finished what they're doing and I can see him again.'

Jenny nodded. 'I shouldn't think they'll be long.'

'You can go in now, Sarah.' Jenny was surprised to see it was Max. He must have come across to the unit earlier.

'Do you want me to come in with you?'

Sarah hesitated, then shook her head. 'I'd rather go alone.'

Jenny scribbled down her phone number. 'If you want to talk to someone, you can reach me there.'

Jenny walked to the door of the unit with Sarah, then, nodding to Max, headed for the changing room. He fell into step beside her. 'Your son will think he's been abandoned.'

'He'll be OK.'

'Would you like me to ring the nursery and let them know you're on your way?'

She stared at him blankly for a moment, then remembered their earlier conversation. 'It's no problem, really. But thanks for the offer. See you tomorrow.'

She made her way into the changing room, totally bemused by his obvious concern for her child. *His* child. And he'd never met him. Why, oh why hadn't she trusted him? Her only excuse was the short time she had known him. She should have told him about the pregnancy and let him make his own mind up about the future.

Instead she was still keeping him at arm's length and now he had turned to Rosie. In any case, how could she tell him that Jamie was his son? Now she'd had time to get to know him a lot better, she was pretty sure he would never forgive her for the lost years.

Jenny spent a restless night of regret and indecision. The one thing that would resolve the situation was impossible. She couldn't move to another hospital. She had to stay in the area for her son's sake. And her mother would want to move with her, and that was not on. She had done enough for Jenny already, and it would be cruel to move her away from her friends.

And what about Rosie? Although every time she saw her with Max Jenny's heart twisted uncomfortably, she had tried hard to convince herself that their friendship would make her own working relationship with Max easier. Maybe back on the same footing it had been at Rexford.

She told herself she was fretting unnecessarily about his concern for her late arrival at Jamie's nursery. It wasn't personal. He would have made the same offer to any of his colleagues who were working late if he'd known they had family commitments.

It was time she stopped thinking of him purely in relation to herself. She was nothing special to him. Just because she'd worked with him before, and they'd had a brief relationship, it didn't mean he thought of her exclusively.

The workload waiting when she arrived on duty next morning wiped all thought of Max from her mind.

'There are four on trolleys in the cubicles, waiting for beds, and it's standing-room only in the waiting room. Max was right. We're making up for those quiet nights. And some.' Donna yawned widely. She had clearly had a bad night.

'Don't, Donna, please,' Jenny gasped as she yawned herself, 'or we'll never get through the hand-over. Now, what wants doing first?'

'We need beds. Urgently. Max and Rosie are coping in the resus room, but we're desperate for cubicle space. Perhaps you could ring Andy and tell him to get his finger out.'

'If he's in yet. *And* not at a meeting.'

The moment the hand-over was completed Jenny lifted the handset and rang the manager's number. Getting no reply, she was about to replace it when the man himself walked into the office. 'Am I glad to see you—'

'Where's Max?'

'Up to his eyes, and I need you to find some beds for the patients clogging up the department.'

Andy rolled his eyes. 'Beds! That's all you people think about. My job has many other priorities, and at the moment one of them demands I have a quick word with Max before I do anything else. I need to warn him.'

Jenny frowned. 'About what?'

'Remember I told you about the friend of the young man who died from the stab wounds making a complaint?'

She nodded.

'Well, now he's found a litigation-happy solicitor.'

Jenny shook her head in despair and said quietly. 'It's ridiculous. Nothing could be further from the truth. I was there.'

'Do you think I doubt that? But Max needs to know what's happening because this idiot has alerted the press. One unguarded word could cause all kinds of trouble.'

'For Max? Or is it the hospital's reputation you're more concerned about? Because if that's the case you'd better start finding some beds. And quick.'

Jenny knew she was being provocative, but lack of sleep was making her unduly critical of the manager.

He assumed a wounded expression and shrugged. 'My, my—cynical, aren't we, this morning? Quite uncalled for, even though I don't know Max as well as you do.' The look that accompanied his words told her Andy must suspect their earlier relationship had been less than platonic, and an uncomfortable flush rose in her cheeks. 'Of course the reputations of the hospital *and* your department are important, but I didn't think you of all people would accuse me of not supporting my staff.'

Remembering how only the day before he had said visiting her department cheered him up, she was about to apologise when he continued, 'And I *have* found beds for all the patients waiting to be admitted.' He slammed a list down onto her desk and stalked out of the office before she could reply.

Jenny groaned as she set about organising admissions into the beds listed. What had possessed her to be so tetchy? She'd always got on well with Andy, but it had taken just ten days of Max's presence in the department for her to blow that.

As soon as she had a free moment she would have to apologise and tell the manager she was having a bad day and hadn't meant a word of what she'd said.

But why was she having a bad day? She couldn't really blame her lack of sleep. She'd had plenty of experience of that when Jamie was younger and it hadn't resulted in her behaving so badly. There must be another reason. Reluctantly she admitted to herself she knew what it was. Jealousy! She was jealous of Rosie.

Brushing aside the uncomfortable thought, she immersed herself in the needs of her patients. Once she'd supervised the removal of those waiting for admission, she joined Annette at the minor end of the unit.

'Any problems?'

Annette shook her head. 'But no free cubicles. I'm waiting for one of the docs to come out of resus to see most of these. Leanne's dealing with what she can in triage to prevent the numbers getting out of hand.'

Jenny nodded and went to see if she could free one of the doctors from the resus room.

'Niall and Rosie can cope here now,' Max told her. 'I'll come and take a look at some of those waiting.'

As they made their way to the patient cubicles she told Max what Andy had said. He shook his head. 'What a waste of time. I contacted my union yesterday and they want a written report on what happened. There goes my free day tomorrow, I guess.'

When, much later, on they had a short break for coffee, he asked, 'Have you heard how Patrick's doing today?'

'No. I'll ring through when I get a minute. That's the only thing I don't enjoy about working in A & E—you rarely hear the eventual outcome unless you make an effort.'

'Perhaps as well,' he laughed. 'If the ones we do know about cause us this much trouble!'

Throughout the rest of the day they worked together well, and Jenny was left to make her way home regretting more than ever the many opportunities she had missed to unburden herself about her son.

Max made himself a strong coffee, hoping to compensate for a disturbed night. He was actually sorry that it was his free day—and it wasn't the hectic workload he was missing, but seeing Jenny. The previous day she had been like the Jenny he first knew, and they had got through a tremendous number of patients between them.

He'd roughed out his report on the stabbed youth the evening before, but during the night he'd kept remembering small details that he wanted to add. So this morning, which should have been the first of two days of freedom, he was rewriting the whole thing.

When he'd finished he sealed and stamped the envelope and set out for the town of Catonbury. He'd have loved to get right away from his flat, but it wasn't possible as he was on call for the next couple of nights. So to pass the rest of the morning he decided to take another look at the estate agents' windows.

Again he found nothing remotely interesting, so wandered into the nearest department store to buy some socks and a couple of shirts.

He was watching the crowds from the balcony restaurant in the small store when he saw a familiar figure on the shop floor below. He was sure it was the little lad he had picked up in the park, and his curiosity made him want to see if the same adult was him.

And if so, to discover if she really was Jenny's relation. Or if his thoughts were so full of her that his mind was playing tricks and conjuring up images of her where they didn't exist.

Leaving his undrunk coffee, he raced down the stairs to find them, but they were lost in the crowds. He shrugged and walked more slowly up the stairs to find his coffee had been cleared away. Rather than bother to queue for another one, he made his way out into the fresh air. It definitely wasn't his morning!

Making his way back through the park, he spotted the youngster again, and he settled on a bench to watch as they approached. He tried not stare, although it wasn't easy when he was so curious, but at least his eyes were hidden by his sunglasses.

As they drew almost level excitement tempted him to leap up and confront them—because he wasn't imagining things. She *was* an older version of Jenny, which surely must make her a close relative—even her mother.

The only thing that stopped him making a fool of himself was the boy. He'd been right about him as well. He was three, at least, so there was no way this could be Jenny's son, but the likeness between the two women certainly was uncanny.

A couple of times he met the woman's eyes watching him and realised he was worrying her. She didn't like him just sitting there looking at them. Perhaps she thought he was one of those men who preyed on children in the park. Max knew there had been warnings about a couple of attempted snatchings in the town over the past couple of weeks.

The woman grasped Jamie's hand more tightly and rushed him on. Away from any danger. Max moved away as well, feeling soiled that anyone might have thought of him in that way. He sighed deeply. Moving to Catonbury had been an appalling mistake.

'I've decided I'm not going to take Jamie to the park any more.' The little boy was in bed and Jenny and her mother were clearing away the remnants of their evening meal.

'Why ever not, Mum? I thought you said he loves it there.'

'I know, but there was a character in there who worried me.'

Jenny frowned. 'In what way?'

'This morning he just sat and stared at him. He didn't seem able to take his eyes off Jamie and I don't like it. I'm pretty sure he's the chap who picked Jamie up that day he grazed his chin. I even saw him looking down on us from the balcony in Browns. I'm beginning to wonder if I should go to the police. If I keep Jamie away he may well go after another child.'

'What does he look like?'

'Tall. Taller than me, anyway. I do remember that. And he always seems to wear sunglasses. I hate that, and it means I never get a good look at him.'

'But you think he's the man who picked Jamie up?'

'He could be, but that day I was paying more attention to Jamie than to him.' She thought for a moment. 'Perhaps I should have said something to him this morning. Let him know I'd seen him.'

'I don't think that's a good idea. I shouldn't let him stop Jamie enjoying the park and the playground, though. As long as you're with him he's safe enough.'

She said no more to her mother, but the way life was playing tricks on her at the moment Jenny decided there was more than a remote possibility that it *could* have been Max who picked him up. She had an idea he had been off duty that day, and it was around that time that he'd checked once or twice how old Jamie actually was. If she was right, the unusual colour of Jamie's eyes would have given him food for much thought. Because there was no doubt about it. They were exactly the same as Max's own.

Had he put two and two together and guessed she hadn't told him the whole truth? It could explain why he kept on at her for answers, and why he was so worried about her always getting to the nursery school on time.

As the thoughts went round and round in her head she tried to dismiss them as ridiculous, but she knew stranger coincidences had happened. And yet, if he *had* worked it out, surely he wouldn't have kept silent. That wasn't Max's way at all. Unless—unless he wasn't telling her the whole truth about his reason for being here.

No. He must just like children. If it *was* Max. She slept eventually, but awoke determined to resolve the problem one way or another. Over breakfast she interrogated her mother. 'That day when Jamie fell in the park and hurt his chin?'

'Yes?'

'You said you thought it was a doctor picked him up?'

'Ye-es?' Her mother frowned.

'He was walking in the direction of the hospital, anyway.'

'Can you remember what he looked like?'

'He was tall. Like the man I described yesterday. I do remember that.' She thought for a moment. 'I can't say I saw much of his face. I suppose he did push his sunglasses up to take a look at the graze, but I'm sure they were back in place again by the time I'd comforted Jamie and looked up to say thank you. I don't believe I could pick him out in an identity parade. Except by his height. He towered over me.'

'I don't think that would help, Mum. Most people are taller than you!' Jenny teased.

She said no more to her mother that morning, but she was uneasy. Maybe Max had noticed the similarity between himself and Jamie and had gone back for a second look. If she was right, and it seemed she must be, it was almost inevitable that he'd ferret out the truth some way—and she preferred to be the one who told him.

She would need to pick her moment and her words carefully, though. His relationship with Rosie appeared to be going from strength to strength, and she needed to reassure him she didn't want or expect anything from him. If he hadn't turned up to work at the hospital the situation would never have arisen, but she now recognised she could put it off no longer.

That evening she spoke to her mother. 'I've given a lot of thought to what you told me this morning, and I don't think there's any danger in you going to the park from now on.'

'Oh, I don't know. I'm still tempted to tell the police—'

Jenny shook her head emphatically. 'No, Mum. Leave it with me. I'm pretty sure I know who it is.'

'You know? How?'

'Shall I describe him for you? Six foot plus tall, with dark wavy hair, and under his jacket he wears a fancy waistcoat?'

'Yes, that's right—I forgot about that. How did you know?'

'Because I have just described Jamie's father. The waistcoat is to house his grandfather's fob watch—something he's very proud of. He's worn a similar one since I first knew him. He considers it the trademark of a successful surgeon.'

Her mother's mouth fell open as she echoed, 'Father? His father. *Jamie's* father…'

Jenny nodded, ruefully aware that her mother had heard nothing she'd said but the word 'father'.

'Jamie's dad… He's here… In Catonbury?'

'I'm afraid so.'

'So why haven't you brought him home to meet Jamie?'

'It's not that easy, Mum.'

'But—but surely he'd love to meet his son.'

Jenny hid an anguished face in her hands for a long moment. 'He probably would, but… Well, at the moment he doesn't know about Jamie—although what you've told me suggests he's probably suspicious.'

'He's your new consultant, isn't he? I knew it was something more than a change of staff bothering you.'

Jenny nodded reluctantly. 'He is, yes. But—and I mean this most sincerely, Mum—you have to keep out of this. I'll tell him when it's the right moment, and if he wants to see Jamie I'll introduce him as my new boss.'

'But—but surely once he knows he'll want the boy to know he's his father?'

'Maybe, but I don't. He's only at the hospital for a short time, and when he moves on Jamie will be the one to suffer. That wouldn't be fair.'

'But if he knew—perhaps he wouldn't move on.'

'That wouldn't be fair to Max. That's his name, by the way. He's had his career planned out since I first knew him, and I would hate to be responsible for him not achieving it. It was my fault I got pregnant, and sure as eggs is eggs he would come to hate both of us for it.'

'But if he married you…'

'That's out of the question, Mum.'

'But you'd move around with him and there'd be no question of spoiling his career.'

She gave her mother a weak smile. 'If I thought he loved me I'd jump at the chance, but I know he doesn't. Even while our affair was going on he had a steady relationship in the background, and when he discovered she was ill, she was the only one he thought about. He didn't contact me once, or return any of my phone calls, so I'm as surprised as you are that he's appeared now—but I do know it's not because he loves me.'

'But…' Her mother was struggling to come to terms with the unexpected news.

'I'm not prepared for him to marry me because he feels he ought to support Jamie. I'm perfectly capable, and I'd rather keep my memories of our happy days together than have us destroy one another. Believe me, I've seen the results of shotgun marriages often enough at the hospital.'

'Is he the reason for your sudden decision to go on holiday?'

'Partly. And partly because I do need a break.'

'I don't know what to say.'

'Just say nothing. That's all I ask. Please, Mum.'

'But it's so unfair—to both of them.'

'I realise it's unfair to Max, but what Jamie never knows he won't miss.'

'I can see why he kept staring at us.'

Jenny nodded. 'I think it's probably the colour of Jamie's eyes that gave it away. Every time I look at Jamie it's like looking at his father.'

Jenny knew it wasn't easy for her mother to understand. In her day if a girl got pregnant her only solution was to marry the father. But not today. Women could support themselves and their children rather than endure a loveless marriage.

*   *   *

'Can I have a word, Max?'

'Sure. As long as I get a coffee with it.'

When she had made the coffee and seated herself safely behind her desk Max took the seat opposite her, and before she could say anything asked, 'Do you think I could meet your son some time?'

His eyes never left her face as she sought for the words she needed. Every muscle in her body tightened with fear. It was now or never. She had to tell him. It was tempting to agree without letting him know the truth, but the instant he saw Jamie he would know she had lied, and he only had to do a simple calculation to work out that the child was his. And the eyes. They were the real giveaway.

'I think you ought to listen to what I have to say first. But I don't think this is the right time and place. Perhaps we could meet up this evening.'

'This evening?'

'What I have to say is not easy.'

He frowned. 'Why? Why won't you let me meet him?'

She realised he hadn't really taken on board what she was saying, rather was waiting for an answer to his earlier question. She was saved from replying by the telephone ringing. Relieved, she lifted the receiver.

It was her mother. 'Hi, Mum,' she greeted her warmly, indicating with her hands and a grimace that she would probably be a little while.

Max took the hint and left, closing the door behind him.

'I've found a last-minute holiday available in Majorca, if you can get the time off. Starting Monday week. Self-catering flat with a pool. Can you let me know as soon as possible?' Her mother gave the information quickly, aware that Jenny had little time to spare at work.

'I'll get back to you as soon as I can, Mum. It'll be

great to get away, and Jamie will love it. I can't wait to spend time with him.'

The senior nursing officer reassured her there was no problem arranging cover for that week. 'You couldn't have chosen a better time, Jenny. Because all the schools are back there's no one else off that week.'

It couldn't have been a better time for her, either. She would tell Max, and then whisk Jamie away until he had got used to the idea. She rang her mother back to confirm, and felt a surge of childish excitement at the thought of time away from the department and Max.

This soon disappeared when she saw the child Leanne was taking into the nearest empty cubicle. She checked on the board and didn't recognise the name Leanne had entered—Kyle Berwin. But she was sure it was the little boy she had queried might have suffered a non-accidental injury.

With an effort, she remembered his name had also been Kyle—but not Berwin, that was wrong. Smith. That was it. Kyle Smith, he'd been called. She recognised his mother as well. She retrieved his earlier record card and joined Leanne in the cubicle.

'This kiddie needs to be moved to the resus room, and quickly,' Leanne greeted her. 'Come with us as well, Mum.'

'What's the problem?' Jenny asked her colleague quietly as they wheeled the trolley across.

'He was apparently climbing on the windowsill and fell heavily onto a cupboard below. He seems very shocked, and has bruised his right side quite badly. There's a fair bit of swelling as well. I think he may have ruptured his spleen.'

Quickly aware of the urgency, Max and Rosie initiated

treatment for shock as the little lad's condition was deteriorating fast.

Jenny murmured, 'I'll get the paediatric registrar and alert the operating theatre.'

By the time the registrar arrived they had sent blood for crossmatching and set up an infusion to combat the loss of fluid in the boy's system. Jenny persuaded the mother to sign her consent and within minutes he was transferred to the operating theatre for an exploratory operation.

Jenny took his mother to the relatives' room to explain what they were doing and where Kyle would go after he left the theatre. Then she said quietly, 'I remember you in here the other day. But you used a different name. You said the little boy was called Kyle Smith. Your address was different as well.'

'I've never been here before. Don't know what you're talking about.' The boy's mother, if that was who she was, flung open the door and flounced down the corridor. 'I've never been in this hospital before.' Then she brazenly made her way to the children's ward to await the boy's return.

Jenny knew she wasn't mistaken. The moment Rosie was free she called her into the office. 'Do you remember the other day I queried if a little boy's injury was accidental?'

Rosie frowned. 'Vaguely.'

'That little boy who went to Theatre with the abdominal bruising—I think he's the same boy. Different name. Which makes me even more suspicious. Did you recognise him?'

Rosie shook her head. 'Not with any certainty. Toddlers all look the same to me. You spend more time with the patients than I do. Who was triage nurse that day?'

'Unfortunately I was doing both. I'm worried about that kiddie, Rosie. It looked to me as if he'd been kicked.'

'Ring the GP. See if they know anything.'

'Depends what his real name is, and which practice they're registered with—if any. Everything they've told us might be false.'

'You can but try. The little lad won't be going home for a few days, so perhaps that will give us a chance to investigate before we discuss it with the powers-that-be. It's up to them to decide what action to take.'

Jenny had to be satisfied with that for the moment, but she was determined not to let the matter drop. She couldn't bear the thought of knowing a child was suffering at the hands of an adult and doing nothing about it.

Of course the practice named on both record cards had no child of either name on the list. 'Difficult, really,' the practice manager told Jenny. 'We have six doctors at this health centre, so I can't ask them all to visit the hospital and try to identify him. Perhaps a health visitor or social worker would be a better bet.'

Max was concerned, but agreed all they could do was report what they suspected. Later, when they were alone again in the office, he said, 'It's always difficult to know if we have a problem in these cases or not. I guess child rearing is not easy and every parent does it differently. Take you, for instance. I asked you earlier about meeting your son, but you seem to keep him under wraps, for some reason.'

'Under wraps?' She laughed nervously. 'I don't know what you mean.'

'No one I've spoken to here has seen him, and you—'

'Why should they? He's part of my private life.'

'You're the only mother I know who doesn't talk about her child. Most do it incessantly.'

'I'm not any mother, thank you. I happen to feel—'

'Are you ashamed of him?'

'Of course I'm not.'

'What about his father? No one seems to know who he is. I don't believe he's free to live with you, is he?'

'Max, I don't know what you're trying to say, but I don't want to discuss it at this moment. I've told you there is something we need to talk about, but I'm not prepared to do it here, where we can be disturbed at any moment.'

He raised his hands in mock surrender. 'OK. As soon as I can get away this evening I'll kill two birds with one stone. I'll come to your house and we can talk—after I've met your son.'

'No. That's the last place I want it to be.'

'I thought not. You don't want me to meet the child's father, do you?'

'Max.' Frustration made her almost shriek his name. 'Stop jumping to conclusions.'

He'd clearly got the bit between his teeth and was as determined to get an explanation from her as she was to give one when the time was right.

He leapt to his feet and grasped her arm roughly. 'Is he married? Is that the problem?'

Jenny experienced a bitter disappointment that he thought so little of her that he could believe she'd behave in that way. But she supposed she couldn't blame him for wanting to know who it was bringing the boy up if he suspected he was the real father.

'Jamie's usually in bed by seven-thirty. Suppose we met for a drink after that.'

'I'm looking for somewhere better to rent while I'm at Catonbury. An agent contacted me today with details of a place that's just come on the market, but it will be snapped up if I don't make a decision this evening. I have

an appointment for seven-thirty, so we could get something to eat when I've seen it and then adjourn to my
present abode for coffee and a chat. It's pretty horrid, but
it'll be private.'

Jenny wasn't sure she wanted to be quite as private as
that, but their talk couldn't wait. Hopefully they'd be able
to talk over the meal.

Sarah popped her head round the office door a few
moments later. 'I thought you'd like to know that
Patrick's been moved out of ITU.'

'Sarah! How wonderful. How is he?'

'Getting it together slowly.'

'I must pop over and see him.'

'He'd like that. He's in the neuro ward, and they say
there's no reason why he shouldn't eventually return to
his job.'

'That's great news, Sarah. I really will try and find a
moment to pop over and see him tomorrow.'

'There's no need for that. I know you're busy but I just
had to thank you for everything you did, Sister. I don't
know how we'll ever repay you.'

Jenny smiled. 'Patrick back to normal will be payment
enough.'

The flat Max saw that evening was even worse than the
place he was in at present.

'The estate agents up here should take to writing fic-
tion,' he told Jenny as they made their way across the
road to the pub. 'This one sounded just what I was looking
for.'

When they'd settled at a table in the corner, and Max
had brought the drinks, she read through the sheet of details and told him, 'They don't mention any bad points,
but I suppose you wouldn't expect them to—'

'Hello, you two. Mind if I join you?'

She heard Max groan beneath his breath before saying, 'Not at all, Dan. Are you eating as well?' In an obvious attempt to allay Dan's suspicions, Max explained, 'I'm treating Jenny to a meal in return for her advice on a new place for me to live.'

Dan's presence made it impossible for them to talk while they ate, and he seemed reluctant to leave even when the meal was finished. When he asked about coffee Jenny shook her head, and, catching Jenny's eye, Max suggested he ran her home.

Once they were in the car, he said, 'Methinks our admin assistant has a thick skin. I was trying to avoid adjourning to my flat, but I can see it's the only place we're going to have some peace.'

'I can see why you want to move,' Jenny told him as she surveyed the two hard-backed dining chairs that were the only place to sit.

Once he had poured coffee for them both he settled on the other chair and asked, 'Now, what's the great secret?'

Unsure where to begin, she looked down at the table.

'Don't look so tragic.' He leaned forward on his chair and kissed her lightly, oh, so lightly, on the lips.

'I know you must have wondered why I made such a mess of that interview I was supposed to walk.'

'Well, yes. But these things happen. We all have bad days.'

She shook her head. 'It was more than that.' She continued with a rush, 'That morning, just before the interview, I did a pregnancy test. It was positive.'

CHAPTER SIX

Max lifted his head sharply. 'What?' He shook his head, as if unable to take in what she was saying. 'You were pregnant?'

Compressing her lips, she nodded, unable to meet his eyes.

'Over three years ago? What are you trying to say? What—? Oh, God, no. Not that.' She saw utter despair in his eyes before he groaned and closed them, resting his head in his hands. 'Not that.'

Jenny felt her heart plummet at his reaction and gave silent thanks that she'd had the sense not to tell him all those years ago. 'I'm sorry—'

'You're sorry?' he spluttered. 'You killed my child and all you can say is you're sorry?'

Appalled at what he'd assumed, she shook her head, 'No, Max. No. That's not what I'm trying to tell you. I didn't—I couldn't have had an abortion.'

He stared at her, as if unable to comprehend what she was saying. 'So—?'

'Yes.' Jenny was too anxious to wait until he worked it out for himself. 'Jamie is…' She faltered, unable to voice the stark truth, and said instead, 'I mean—I told you lies about the age of my son.'

He stared at her as he tried to make sense of what she was telling him. 'Are you telling me I'm his father?'

She nodded. Then, stealing a glance at his face, couldn't believe the mix of emotions that she read there.

Disbelief and despair were mingled with an emerging wonder at the news.

He shook his head. 'I can't believe it. Here was I, thinking perhaps his father was married, or in some way not free… Oh, Jenny. I can't take this in.' He continued to shake his head.

Wishing he would give some indication as to how he felt about being a father, she murmured, 'I'm sorry. I thought you'd guessed. I thought that was why you've been watching him in the park.'

'Watching?' He frowned. 'Of course. The little boy. I admit I took a second look, but I certainly haven't made a habit of it. How did you know, anyway?'

'My mother's description. You picked him up when he fell a few days ago, didn't you?'

He nodded. 'But this was the last thing I imagined.'

'So what was your interest in him?'

'His grandmother. You two look so alike I knew she had to be your mother, and I was fascinated. And, I have to admit, puzzled. The boy was too grown-up for a two-year-old.'

'I thought it was his eyes.'

He frowned. 'His eyes?'

She nodded. 'They're exactly like yours. The colour, I mean.'

'I didn't notice that— I want to meet him as soon as possible.'

'Max…' She sighed. 'That's what I want to talk to you about. I don't think it's a good idea for him to know—'

He leaned across the table and grasped her shoulders. 'You don't… I can't believe what I'm hearing. You've kept knowledge of my son from me all this time and now you don't think it's a good idea—'

'Max! Please listen. I've had a long time to think this

through. I'm very happy for you to spend time with him while you're at Catonbury, but not for him to know you're his father.'

His face black with fury, he demanded, 'So what do you suggest?'

'I was going to suggest I introduce you as a work colleague.'

He leapt to his feet, sending his chair toppling backwards, and Jenny shrank back in her seat. 'I don't believe this.'

'Max, please. Let me explain. You've already said you won't be staying in Catonbury. Think what it'll do to him to discover his father only to lose him again.'

He raised his arms helplessly, 'Jenny!' he thundered. 'When I said that, I didn't know I had a son here. This changes the situation completely.'

'I know—'

'We'll get married.'

'No!'

Her vehement refusal stopped him in his tracks, and he righted his chair and sat down again. 'Isn't that why you're telling me?'

'Certainly not.' She was so enraged by his insinuation for a moment she could hardly speak.

'Well, if you don't want to get married, what do you want? Money?'

His words scythed through her so deeply that she had to blink back tears as she said quietly, 'I don't want anything from you, Max. Ever. Neither does Jamie. I'm sorry I told you now. The sooner you get out of our lives again the better.' She snatched up her jacket and made for the door.

He grasped her shoulders. 'Don't go, Jenny. Please. I didn't mean— It was such a shock—not a shock. I don't mean that, either. It was so unexpected, though. I didn't think what I was saying.'

'Your response is exactly what I expected, which is why I didn't tell you when I first knew I was pregnant. We don't need you, Max. We're managing perfectly well as we are.' She opened the door, but when she tried to close it firmly behind her he pulled it open again.

As she made her way down the stairs she heard his anguished whisper, 'Don't leave like this, Jenny.' But she kept on walking.

Aware that he couldn't shout any louder at this time of night, and would have to retrieve his shoes from the kitchen before he could follow her, Jenny made her way out to her car.

What a mess! And the irony of it was that there'd been no need to tell him. He hadn't suspected for a moment that he was Jamie's father. Oh, well, it was done now, and he'd reacted exactly as she had feared when she'd first known she was pregnant.

At least now she knew where she stood, and she had already proved she could cope on her own. How dared he assume she'd only told him about his son because she wanted something from him?

Well, she might still want *him,* but however much she might have once loved Max he had just made it abundantly clear that he had no feelings whatsoever for her. To marry him under those circumstances would be intolerable. And so unfair to Jamie.

She made her way quietly into the house to avoid waking either her mother or her son, and it wasn't until she was safely in bed and her anger began to subside that she allowed her tears to flow uncontrollably. Because, however much she hated to admit it, she *had* nurtured a grain of hope that she might have got him wrong. But she certainly hadn't. He didn't love her and never had. The sooner he moved on and left her to rebuild her shattered dreams the better.

She had been on duty for only a few minutes the next day when Kyle's mother came in search of her.

'Can I see you for a few minutes?'

Jenny looked enquiringly towards Lisa, who was waiting to give her the hand-over report. 'Could you brief Leanne this morning and I'll see her later?'

Clearly puzzled, Lisa agreed, while querying with raised eyebrows if all was well.

Jenny nodded, and told her quietly, 'This lady's little boy was admitted to paeds yesterday.'

Fearing the worst, she led the way to the relatives' room before asking how the little boy was.

'He's doing fine.' Mrs Smith/Berwin burst into floods of tears. 'But you were right. I have been here before. Don't tell the social. Please. They'll take him away, and I couldn't bear that.'

Jenny pulled up two chairs and guided the woman to one of them. 'Now, start at the beginning and tell me what this is all about.'

'I've been worrying all night,' she sobbed. 'I knew you were suspicious, and I couldn't bear them to take him away. He's all I've got.'

Jenny put an arm round her. 'Nobody's going to do anything without giving you a chance to tell your side of the story. Are you trying to tell me Kyle was injured deliberately?'

She sniffed and nodded, but said nothing.

'Who by?'

'His dad. He loves him really, but he loses control when we have a row and takes it out on the lad. I should never have married him. Just because I was pregnant. He's never forgiven me. He'd just met that Sharon from over Wirtly way and he wanted to marry her. He hates me now. Says I trapped him.'

'It takes two to make a baby, Mrs...?' Jenny deliberately left the name blank and waited to see if she would be given the real one.

'Hobson. His real name is Kyle Hobson. I gave the other names because I was frightened. I don't want to lose him.' She broke into a fresh outburst of tears.

'Try and calm down, Mrs Hobson. Would you like some tea? Or coffee?'

'Tea, please. Two sugars.'

'I'll be back in a moment.'

Jenny sped to the office and thankfully found Leanne there. 'Could you ring paeds and see what, if anything, is being done about that little lad you saw yesterday? You know what I'm talking about, don't you?' At Leanne's nod, she added, 'I'm just going to get tea for his mother, then I'll pop back.'

When she discovered no one had been alerted about the injuries because his correct name and address weren't known, she thanked Leanne and said she hoped to be out to help within ten minutes.

It was nearer twenty before Mrs Hobson was sufficiently reassured to return to her son's bedside. Jenny saw her in the right direction, promising to go and see her again later.

Max was with Leanne in the office when Jenny went to find out where she was needed. He watched her closely. She knew he was trying to catch her eye and pretended not to notice. She knew only too well what he wanted. He was no doubt bursting to talk to her. But he would have to wait. As she had driven to work in the chilly dawn it had become clear to her that now she had blurted out the truth she couldn't leave it there. She would have to let Max meet Jamie. But not as his father.

Leanne asked, 'Difficult, was she?'

Jenny started, having momentarily forgotten about Kyle and his mother. 'Er—not really. More pathetic than anything. I think we need to convene a meeting with the paeds lot as soon as possible. She's scared we'll report her and the lad will be taken away.'

'It *was* non-accidental, then?'

It was the first time Max had spoken, and after what Mrs Hobson had confided Jenny's response was guarded. 'That's something we need to discuss further. She's obviously a caring mother, who loves him dearly, but she may need help to cope.'

'You mean she loses her rag and—'

Jenny cut short Max's exasperated query. 'I'm not saying that at all, Max. I don't think it's anything to do with her. But I've only heard her side of the story. She blames her husband, but says he is moving out. All this will need checking if we are to prevent serious injury to Kyle in the future. I'm just querying whether it is better for him to stay in an environment where he is loved rather than one where there is no mum to love him.'

'You're suggesting we leave him at risk of more battering, then?'

'Of course not. All I'm saying is that the future risk does need assessing so that the wrong decision isn't made. It's all too easy to remove a child and regret it later. That's precisely why I'm suggesting an all discipline discussion.' Jenny guessed he had read the irritation in her voice at what she considered his deliberate misunderstanding. 'I'll try and arrange it immediately.'

'On a Sunday? Are you sure you're not letting your own feelings colour the situation?'

It took all the professional restraint Jenny could muster not to launch into the verbal attack she had spent the night wishing she had delivered the previous evening. But she wasn't prepared to let him get away with it completely. Instead she retorted coolly, 'There's always an emergency social worker on call.'

'Yep. And she'll be pulled in so many directions that it'll be at least midnight until she's free. You know that as well as I do.'

She shrugged. 'We don't know that until we try.'

She lifted the receiver and Leanne, who had followed the to and fro nature of their exchange as if watching a tennis match, took the opportunity to escape. 'I must have patients to see by this time.'

Determined not to enter a discussion with Max about Jamie until she was sure they wouldn't be interrupted, Jenny looked pointedly at Max. 'Shouldn't you be seeing patients as well?'

'Rosie'll let me know if they can't cope. Jenny, I need to talk to you.'

'Later.' She banged down the receiver. 'They're not answering and this can't wait. Kyle's mother isn't likely to tell anyone else what she told me.' She pulled open the office door.

Max grasped her arm to detain her. 'Isn't the future of *our* son important to you?'

'Of course it is, Max, but not at this precise moment. Perhaps we can discuss this after work. Or at lunchtime.'

He released his hold and she was aware of him following her out of the office. When she turned to check the numbers in the waiting area she caught sight of his thunderous expression and knew that before they met up again she must know exactly what she was going to say to him.

One thing was for certain: Mrs Hobson's plight had reinforced her decision that a marriage between two people just because they'd created a baby was not likely to succeed. Especially if one partner resented being trapped.

Love was needed on both sides to weather the ups and downs of any marriage and she was not prepared to accept anything less just because Max was Jamie's father.

It took her the whole morning to persuade most of the interested parties that it was important to meet up for the sake of Kyle, but she had to admit Max was right. It wouldn't be until the next day as Kyle was in no immediate danger.

When she had a moment she would have a longer chat with the staff on the children's ward, and with Kyle's mum.

In between her deliberations she was able to see some of the patients waiting in the minor end of the department, which kept her well away from Max, who was busy in the resuscitation area.

To her relief, when lunchtime came they were so busy that none of them was able to take a proper lunch break. Fran brought an assortment of sandwiches from the canteen and they consumed them as and when they were able.

Whenever their paths crossed, Jenny was aware of Max watching her closely. She was about to leave for her chat with the paediatric staff when he found her snatching a quick cup of coffee in the office.

He closed the door behind him. 'How long before you'll be free?'

She shrugged. 'I've no idea.'

'Is it easier for you to find time to talk when you finish here, or later this evening?'

She knew he was giving her the choice to prevent her finding a reason not to meet up, and was perversely tempted to say neither, but she didn't want him arriving at the house without prior warning and it was obvious he wasn't prepared to wait any longer.

'I'd rather get home and see Jamie to bed, then meet you for a drink.'

'And some food?'

She would have preferred just the drink, but guessed he wouldn't have eaten. 'OK.'

'I'll pick you up about eight, then. The Cricketers OK?'

'No.' Her response was vehement as she pictured him charming her mother onto his side before she had a chance to sort something out.

'I don't mean the pub. The Cricketers is fine, but I'll drive. I won't be drinking.' No way. She needed a clear mind for what lay ahead. 'Do you want me to call for you?'

'I'll walk.' His reply was curt and she knew he was annoyed that she'd prevented him going to her house.

'That's fine by me.'

The informal chat about Kyle dragged on long past Jenny's normal finishing time, but after her reassurance to Kyle's mum she was determined the little boy wasn't going to be removed from her care unless it was absolutely necessary. She understood the concern. After much bad press medical staff and social workers tended to err on the side of safety for the child, and she couldn't blame them, but this time she felt there was a chance it wasn't necessary.

When the meeting ended Jenny slipped into the family room of the children's ward, where she found Mrs Hobson alone. She explained what was happening, then asked, 'How's things?'

'He's a lot better. Asleep at the moment.'

'I've done what I can. Hopefully a social worker will be able to get into contact with your husband tomorrow, and if he confirms he's moving out I should think there's a good chance that Kyle will be able to stay with you. But it'll be under strict supervision.'

'I don't mind that. I just don't want to lose him.' She grabbed her hand gratefully. 'Thank you, Sister. Thank you.'

'If that's what's agreed, what happens from then on is up to you.'

Mrs Hobson nodded. 'I won't let you down, Sister.'

Jenny smiled. 'It's Kyle you mustn't let down. Take care of him, and if you need to talk at any time you know where I am.'

They shook hands and, only too conscious that she was letting her own son down by working so late, Jenny made her way home as quickly as she could.

Her mother greeted her with a welcome cup of tea. 'Jamie's fine. He's eaten and had his bath. He's in bed, waiting for you to read him a story.'

'Thanks, Mum. You're a star. And I'm deserting you again this evening, I'm afraid. I'm sorry, but I'll be eating out. I wouldn't go if it wasn't important.'

She nodded thoughtfully. 'To do with work?'

'Yes. No. Well, partly.'

'Jamie's dad? Max, is it?'

Jenny groaned. 'Whatever gives you that idea?'

'Is that a yes?'

Jenny sighed deeply, then nodded. 'He wants to meet Jamie, but we need to get a few things straight first.'

'Good. I do think Jamie ought to know his father.'

'No, Mum. He can meet him, but he's not to know who Max is.'

'Why ever not?'

'This is our business, Mum. Mine and Max's. You're not to say anything. I mean it, Mum.'

As soon as Jamie was asleep, Jenny sorted through some photographs of her son. She found one of the best and slipped it into her handbag, then, without paying any attention to what she was wearing, she swilled water round her face, applied a minimum of lipstick and left.

But not before she had once again thanked her mother and warned her, 'Don't forget what I said, will you? Jamie mustn't know Max is his father.'

Her mother nodded and followed Jenny to the door. 'I'll go along with that. For the moment. But it's under protest.'

Jenny climbed into her car, wishing Max had never come to Catonbury. Life had been so simple until that morning he'd appeared in the department. She was even at odds with her mother. Something she'd never known before, even as a teenager.

Max came into the crowded car park to meet her as she pulled up outside the pub.

'I didn't expect it to be so busy. I'm afraid you're going to have to park in the village car park and walk back across the green. I'll come with you.' He opened her passenger door and climbed in beside her, but when he would have kissed her on the lips she averted her head at the last minute so that it landed on her cheek.

The green was crowded with children playing cricket, football and what looked like a combination of both.

'I've booked a table outside, if that's all right by you?'

She nodded.

'How was Kyle?'

'He's progressing well.'

He grinned. 'Useful medic speak.'

'Sorry.'

He took hold of her arm. 'Don't—it's me that should apologise. I was teasing you. Do the ward staff agree with you?'

'I think so. It'd be easy to make the wrong decision without taking all the facts into account.'

'Kyle's future is taking up a lot of your time, Jenny,' he said quietly. 'And it's not really your concern now he's been admitted.'

She pulled her arm free and glared at him. 'I'm the only one his mother has confided in, and—'

'And worrying about Kyle stops you worrying about your own son. Is that it?'

'Of course not. Jamie has always been and still is my number one priority.'

'Mmm. I'll tell you if I agree with that when we've had our chat.'

She stared at him in disbelief. 'He's a happy and well-adjusted little boy. Everyone says so.'

'I don't doubt it.'

She frowned, but they were interrupted by a young girl handing them the menus.

'What would you like to drink, Jen?'

'Diet Coke, please.'

He gave his order, and until they were served she tried to work out how to deal with the demands she knew he was about to make.

The drinks spilled over as they were banged down on the table in front of them.

'I've got some tissues,' she told him as he took out his handkerchief to prevent the liquid running down onto their clothes. 'All mothers carry loads of them!'

He nodded and, clearly not prepared to wait any longer, said, 'Right. Down to business.'

The waitress reappeared and produced a pad and pencil. 'Ready to order?'

Not having looked at the menus, they both quickly perused the specials board she indicated and made their choices.

'Let's get this sorted out before she's back with the food.'

Jenny could see he was becoming increasingly frustrated by the delay and nodded.

'When can I meet my son?'

'I'll arrange for you to meet Jamie, but, as I said, I think it best if he never knows you're his father.'

He shook his head. 'I don't believe this. You don't tell me I have a son for over three years and then you tell me he's not allowed to know I am his father?'

'Keep your voice down, Max, please. Those people in the corner are very interested.'

He ran his outstretched fingers through his hair, then rested his elbow on the table to cup his chin while he regarded her steadily. She thought she could detect tears of rage at the back of his eyes and tried to explain quietly.

'Max, I'm not trying to be unreasonable—'

'Unreasonable?' he spluttered angrily. 'Unreasonable? I...' He didn't continue as she looked furtively around and held her forefinger to her lips.

'I told you, Jamie is happy with the set-up we have now.'

'Well, I'm not.'

'Max! Like I said last night, to have a father come onto the scene and then disappear is likely to upset him, and I'm not prepared to allow it.'

'And I've told you I have no intention of disappearing again.'

'What about your career? You told me you had each step mapped out.'

'Jenny, this is my son we're talking about. Once we're married it won't matter where I work. He'll be with us.'

'But I don't want to get married.'

'Duck for you.' The young girl banged down a plate in front of Max. 'This'll be yours, then,' she said to Jenny, leaning over Max's shoulder to hand her a plate of sea-food salad. 'I'll get your veg,' she told Max.

The moment they were alone again he leaned across the table and tried to reach Jenny's hand. 'Don't you love me, Jenny? I—'

'Here you go, then,' the waitress interrupted, handing Max a dish of vegetables, then obviously hanging around to see if she could hear any more of such an interesting conversation.

Max turned and thanked her with a smile.

'Anything else you need?'

'No, thank you. That's fine.'

Jenny quickly unwrapped her cutlery from her serviette and sighed deeply. Max did the same.

'This wasn't a good idea, was it?'

She shook her head. 'You'd better eat that before it's cold. We can sort this out later.'

Throughout the meal they talked spasmodically about the work of the department and some of the other happenings of the day. When they'd both finished the food in front of them Max offered, 'Dessert? Or coffee? Or both?'

'No, thanks. That was fine. What about you?'

'I know it's not exactly the Ritz, but we could go back to my place again. At least we can talk there without fear of being overheard or disturbed, and I could make some coffee.'

Reluctant to return to the scene of the previous night's confrontation, she said, 'I can't stay long. We could talk as we walk down to the car park.'

'If that's what you'd prefer.'

'I would. It's great to be out in the fresh air after being stuck in that overheated hospital environment.'

'Right. Let's walk. *And* talk.'

He paid the bill and they set off the long way round the green. They walked in silence for a short distance, then Max took her hand and pulled her to a stop. 'I didn't mean all those things I said last night, Jenny. I was shellshocked by your revelation.'

'I *did* break the news rather badly, I'm afraid. I was so sure you'd already guessed.'

He shook his head slowly and started walking again. 'I still can't believe it—and I can't wait to get to know him.'

'I can understand that, and I'm happy to arrange for you too see him whenever it's convenient to you.'

'And you'll tell him I'm his father?'

'No.'

He didn't speak immediately, but the tension in his jaw muscles told her how hard he was finding it to control himself.

She felt compelled to voice her reasons again, but this time calmly and without rancour. 'It wouldn't be fair to Jamie, Max—'

'To get to know his father only to lose him. I know. You've already told me—and I've told you that he won't. I don't *need* to move on, or you can both move with me.'

Jenny stared ahead silently. He made it sound so easy and so tempting, but after seeing at first hand what marriage for the sake of a child could do, she wanted no part of it.

That sort of thing could lead to nothing but unhappiness. Which would upset her as much as Jamie.

'I still think it would probably be best if we meet "by accident" in the park, and I tell him you are someone I work with. We can take it from there and see how it goes.'

'Someone you work with,' Max muttered with contempt. 'Is that all I am to you these days? You do realise that there would be nothing stopping me telling him the truth?'

Jenny stopped dead in her tracks, her horror preventing her from speaking clearly. 'I—you— I don't— You wouldn't—'

He grasped her arm firmly. 'No. I wouldn't. But—'

'No. You won't. Because there's no way now you are ever going to meet him.' Her voice was pure ice. 'Goodnight, Max. Thank you for the meal.' To her relief she saw they'd nearly reached the car, so she spun on her heel and let herself into the driver's seat.

Wrong-footed by her unexpected move, Max arrived at the car as she started the engine. She wound down the window a fraction.

'Jenny—'

'I must get home to *my* son. If you need transport I'm sure the barman'll let you ring for a taxi,' she suggested crisply, and drove from the car park. As she did so his face was reflected momentarily in her rearview mirror, and the look of utter despair she saw there made her want to cry.

Ruefully, Max watched her car out of sight. Why, oh, why hadn't he stayed calm as he had intended? He had behaved in a completely irrational manner. Again. The trouble was that every time he thought of Jamie growing up without knowing his father, he saw red. Good God, was it surprising? He'd missed three years of the boy's life already. It just wasn't fair. He was in the kind of situation he had never in a million years envisaged might arise. He would gladly marry Jenny the next day. He'd wanted her for so long, but clearly she no longer loved or trusted him.

He set out for the short walk home, conscious that every day that passed was one more day he hadn't spent with his son, who was growing up fast. And it hurt. He had to find a way to convince Jenny that he really did love her. Surely she realised that was why he'd taken the job at Catonbury?

He remembered with a sinking feeling Jenny's comments the day before about Rosie. Surely she didn't think—? He groaned. She obviously did. It must look to her as if his affections were so shallow that he could transfer them on a whim.

If he told her about his arrangement with Rosie she would never believe him now. And he couldn't blame her. To salve his pride he'd deliberately not corrected Jenny when she'd assumed he and Rosie had something going together, so if he appeared to drop Rosie now in a bid to marry the mother of his son even he wouldn't blame her for rejecting him. What a hopeless mess he'd got himself into.

Through no fault of his own, either. Jenny had assured him she was on the pill. He couldn't believe she was the sort of person to try and trap him into marriage that way, but what else could he think? The pill was nigh on one hundred per cent effective—unless…unless—had she been taking antibiotics for any reason, or suffered a stomach upset? Whatever had happened, between them they'd created something wonderful, and somehow he had to convince Jenny that he needed them both.

CHAPTER SEVEN

JENNY barely slept that night. She dreaded coming face to face with Max the next morning. Not because she had left him stranded—she wasn't frightened for herself, but for Jamie. However much she tried to prevent it, it would be difficult to stop him meeting up with Jamie if he was determined. In fact it was downright impossible. While she was at work he could call at the house, or make it a coincidental meeting in the park, and there was nothing she could do.

As he was on duty for the next twenty-four hours, she said nothing to her mother before leaving the house. But she knew it would be necessary before his next free day. What was she going to say? Call the police if he approaches you? Don't let him speak to Jamie? It all sounded so petty. Especially when her mother herself thought Jamie ought to know him.

She parked her car and crawled into work, wondering how she would ever last the day Within ten minutes she knew she wouldn't. It was a nightmare scenario. Leanne rang in sick, then Fran. There was standing room only in the waiting room, and along the walls four patients on trolleys waited for a bed to be found for them.

Max and Rosie were trying to resuscitate a young lad who had been drinking the night before and had been found unconscious at the base of a high wall earlier in the morning. He was thought to be suffering from a head injury and exposure, as well as the overdose of alcohol.

'It's a wonder he's still alive,' Max told Jenny quietly. 'Look at these X-rays.'

Jenny gasped as she looked at the injuries and frowned. 'Do you think he was attacked?'

'No one seems to know what happened. The police are trying to get in touch with his family and friends to try and find out. I want to have a word with ITU, so could you take over here for a moment, Jen? He needs constant monitoring. I think he may have taken drugs as well as alcohol.'

'You've sent bloods for analysis, I guess.'

'Mmm.' He nodded as he spoke.

'Hope they can find him a bed, otherwise we'll be stacking the patients.'

'Typical Monday morning,' he muttered as he left the room.

Lunchtime came and went without either of them getting a break, leaving Max exasperated. He'd hardly slept the night before for thinking about the mess he'd made of things. Why, oh, why had he lost his temper? As he'd tossed and turned throughout the night he'd told himself again and again that he should have known it was the worst thing he could do. If her pride had prevented her remaining at Rexford when she hadn't got the job, threatening her in the way he had was downright stupid. Somehow he had to get her to listen to him for long enough to convince her that his son was far too important to him to risk his happiness.

He poured himself a mug of much needed coffee while he waited for some spinal X-rays of a builder who'd fallen from scaffolding. If he could only get enough time alone with Jenny to persuade her to meet him later he would feel as if he had a chance of putting things right, but she'd barely spoken to him all day and when she had it had been work-related. He knew they were busy, but she seemed hell-bent on keeping as far away from him as possible.

Noticing his patient was back, with the X-rays, he downed his coffee and launched himself into the fray again. The X-ray of the cervical spine showed nothing to suggest an injury to the vertebrae, but he still wasn't happy and called the orthopaedic consultant, J.P. for a second opinion.

'His reflexes are present, but sluggish.'

'Where's the lateral view?'

Max handed it to him. 'Can you spot something I'm missing?'

J.P. shook his head. 'I'm not sure. Do you know what caused the fall?'

'Lack of concentration, he says.'

'Mmm.'

'What are you thinking?'

'There are one or two degenerative changes that suggest he could have early cervical spondylosis. How old is he?'

'Er…' Max checked the notes he'd made. 'Fifty-four.'

'Mmm. I'll have a chat with him and then talk to the neuro guys. I'll get back to you. Looks like you've more than enough to cope with out there.'

Max nodded ruefully. 'You can say that again. I hate Mondays.'

Lisa saw he was free and told him Rosie might need help in the resus room.

He found she was coping well without him, so he joined Niall and Annette in seeing the ever increasing number of walking wounded.

When at last the number of patients waiting to be seen began to dwindle, he left the junior doctor to cope and strode up to Jenny's office. After knocking on the closed door, he didn't wait to be invited in. Rosie was seated at her desk, writing up some case-notes.

'Where's Jenny?' he asked abruptly.

Rosie looked up with a puzzled frown. 'You've missed her. She's gone home. Anything I can do?'

He sighed deeply. 'I don't believe it. I've been trying to have a word with her all day.'

'Problem?'

He gestured helplessly. 'Not really, I suppose. I put my foot in it with her yesterday and wanted to apologise.'

'She won't hold a grudge. Not Jenny. I expect she's forgotten about it already.'

'Don't you believe it,' he muttered, and turned to leave the room, aware just how much he wanted to unburden himself but also aware that Jenny would never forgive him if he did.

'Was Jenny the girl you told me about? The one you came looking for and found was in another relationship?' asked Rosie.

He swung round and said, 'You're jumping to conclusions!'

'Perhaps I am. But Jenny did tell me you'd worked together before, and that it was a clash of personality.'

'That's what she said? I would have said it was completely the opposite.'

'Oops. Why don't I keep my big mouth shut?'

He rested a hand on her shoulder. 'Forget it, Rosie. You weren't to know.'

She pushed the telephone towards him. 'Ring her. She should be home by now.'

He shook his head. 'I'll see her tomorrow.'

She came round the desk and gave him a hug. 'Are you off soon? You look bushed. Come round for a meal tonight?'

'No, thanks, love. Not tonight.' He returned her hug to show his appreciation.

A gasp of surprise made him swing round to find Jenny framed in the doorway.

'I'm sorry to interrupt. You obviously thought I'd left, but I was at a meeting.'

'Of course.' He closed his eyes, trying to shut out the horror of what Jenny must be thinking. 'About Kyle, wasn't it? Did it go all right?'

'Fine.' Her voice was cold. 'I came back to see if I was needed, but clearly I'm not. Goodnight.'

She strode off down the corridor. Max hurried after her.

He caught up with her at the door of the changing room. 'Jenny. I've been trying to have a word with you all day—'

'I've been busy.' She pushed the door open.

'Jenny. Please listen.'

'I'm sorry. I'm late already. I have to get back to Jamie.'

'You'd be prepared to stay and work if we were still busy.'

'That's different—important.'

'You're saying our talking isn't?'

She sighed, and after scrutinising him slowly said, 'I don't think anything you have to say is more important than Jamie.'

'I think it is, Jenny,' he told her softly. 'You and I have lives as well, and neither of us can pretend they'll be the same now you've told me about *my* son.' He deliberately emphasised the word. 'That's why I must talk to you.'

She knew he was right, but she was too tired to think about what she wanted to say to him. She needed nothing more at that moment than to go home, shut the door behind her and have an early night.

'You say when and where and I'll be there—but away from here. Talking in this place is hopeless,' he said.

'Could we leave it until tomorrow? Please, Max. I'm bushed.'

'I know. Tomorrow, then. And Jenny?'

'Yes?'

'Whatever I may have said in the heat of the moment yesterday, I didn't mean it. I want you to know that I would never do anything to hurt either you or *our* son.'

She lifted her head to meet his eyes, and in that moment she believed he meant it. 'Thanks.'

She closed the changing room door behind her, strangely relieved. The knowledge that she didn't have to hide Jamie's existence any more had lightened her load considerably, and after that reassurance she didn't think she would mind now even if he demanded regular access. There was surely no way he would be able to fight for custody. The demands of his career would prevent him being there for the boy on a regular enough basis. But still—how could she be so sure?

She pulled up in front of her home feeling physically sick. He'd sounded so sincere a few moments ago. But all the time he could be planning to take the child from her, tear him away from the mother he loved.

She almost fell into the house in her haste to check that Jamie was still there. Safe and sound.

'We're up here, dear,' her mother called from the bathroom. 'We've made some paper boats and we're sailing them in the bath.'

She rushed upstairs without even removing her jacket and hugged a very wet Jamie to her chest.

'Everything all right?' her mother asked with a frown.

'It is now.' She smiled.

'Now?' Her mother was clearly puzzled.

'Now I know Jamie's all right.'

'Why shouldn't he be?'

'Just being a bit silly after things that have happened at work.'

Her mother nodded, obviously still not completely convinced. 'It's a good job you're having a holiday soon. Things seem to be getting on top of you.'

'Not really, Mum. But I am tired, and I'm determined to have an early night.'

'Good idea. Shall we eat with Jamie, then?' At Jenny's nod, her mother said, 'You stay and play with him. I'll do the honours tonight.'

Her mother produced a tasty high tea for them all in a remarkably short time, and the three of them had a happy meal together.

The moment Jamie was asleep, her mother said, 'I'm away to my little den now. There's a film I want to watch on TV.'

Jenny laughed and teased, 'Now I see why the food appeared so quickly. You had it all planned!'

Audrey Stalham laughed. 'Sussed at last!'

Jenny was suddenly serious. 'I really do appreciate what you do for me, Mum. You do a great job with Jamie, and look after me as well. I don't deserve it.' She hesitated.

Her mother didn't wait for her to say more. 'Having you here kept me sane when your dad died. I don't know what I'd have done without you both. It's me who's the lucky one.'

Jenny gave her a warm hug. 'You and me both. But… um…er, Mum?'

'You want to move out?'

'No way. I couldn't manage without you and that's the truth. I've no worries at all about leaving him with you.'

'But?'

'I know it's silly, but I was going to ask you to keep a closer eye on him than usual. I have a feeling Max might try to see him when I'm not around.'

'His father? But surely he should.'

Jenny sighed. 'I suppose so, but I don't want him blurting out the truth to Jamie when he's not prepared. He's such a happy child at the moment. It would be criminal to do that to him.'

'So why don't you tell him yourself? That way you wouldn't have to worry—and his father does have a right. You *do* know that, don't you?'

'Oh, yes. I certainly do,' Jenny responded ruefully. 'I'll have a chat with him tomorrow, to try and work something out…'

'That's good. And if you want to bring him back to the house I'm happy to disappear to my rooms, or even visit a friend.'

Jenny hugged her. 'I don't know what I'd do without you, Mum. I do love you.'

'In that case let me go and watch my film in peace and don't worry. I never let Jamie out of my sight.'

Jenny settled in a comfortable chair with a cup of coffee and mused on what her mother had said. It was easier said than done not to worry. If only she knew exactly what Max wanted. The more she thought about it the more she came to believe that his offer of marriage had been made in the heat of the moment. And if he was prepared to let Clare down by doing that that for the sake of a son he didn't even know, he was a definite force to be reckoned with.

One thing was absolutely certain. She was Jamie's mother and she was the one who was going to bring him up. Whatever plans Max might have, he would have to change them.

Her unhappy thoughts ensured she spent another restless night. She was up early, determined to arrange their chat as soon as possible. Not only for Jamie's sake but her own.

As usual the work of the department intervened. It was an unbelievably hectic morning. But Max was as determined as she was to waste no more time, and demanded they met as soon as they were both able to finish their day's work.

That turned out to be difficult. The continuous flood of patients meant that neither would be able to get away at anything approaching their usual time. Eventually it became clear to Jenny that if they carried on with their plan she would not be home for Jamie's bedtime. Something she tried desperately to avoid.

She decided that the next free moment she had she would go in search of Max.

'Can we postpone our talk until later?' she asked him, when he dashed in for a cup of coffee. 'I like to see Jamie to bed, and at this rate it'll be impossible.'

Max demonstrated his exhaustion by allowing his whole body to sag dramatically. 'Yes, please. I'll need more than a breather when I eventually escape. To save you looking for a babysitter, I could come round to your place. Once Jamie's in bed, that is.'

'No.' Her vehement response was automatic, then she had second thoughts. It would be easier. Her mother had offered to visit a friend and Jamie rarely woke. 'Well, perhaps it would be possible. Can I ring you later?'

He wrote down his mobile number and handed it to her as she scurried away. He frowned after her. Was he missing something? He had an uncomfortable feeling there was something she was still keeping from him. Had his first suspicions been right? Was she living with someone she didn't want him to meet? And his son? If so, did he call him Dad? Was that why Jenny was so insistent that Jamie be told he was a work colleague and nothing more? That thought cut deep, causing a physical pain in his chest. No way was she going to put off this chat a moment longer. He had to know the truth.

Whatever, there wasn't time to think about it now. He finished his coffee and returned to his neglected paperwork, resolving to speak to Andy at the first possible opportunity. In the short time that he had worked there it had become obvious to him that the work of the department had outgrown the current staffing levels, and none of them could continue working for the long hours that were necessary.

He could hardly think straight, Jenny looked exhausted, and stress levels were rising in all the staff. Sick leave would increase unless he could persuade Andy to do something about it. And quickly.

He was interrupted five minutes later by Jenny. 'Major RTA coming in. From the motorway. They should be here any minute.'

'How many?'

'Just the one at that moment. We'll find out from the paramedics if there'll be more.'

'Have we cleared a resus bay?'

Jenny nodded. 'And Rosie's standing by.'

As he followed her along the corridor he could hear the approaching siren, so they were outside and waiting when the ambulance arrived.

Still working on the patient, the paramedic looked up and shrugged. 'Not sure what's happening here, Doc.' As they unloaded the trolley and pushed it through to the resus room he told Max, 'Could have collapsed before ploughing into the central barrier.'

'Heart attack?'

'Don't think so—though he's extremely shocked. There's an abdominal mass.'

'Probably bleeding from an injury.' Max pulled back the sheet to take a look and exclaimed, 'My God, it's an aneurysm. Alert theatres, Jenny and find a surgeon—the more experienced the better. We need more lines in, Rosie, and blood for cross matching. Pronto. Get everyone in here. Any others involved?' he asked the paramedic.

'No. Thank goodness.'

'One-two-three.' Max counted the move onto one of their own trolleys as the surgical registrar joined them. Jenny attached the monitoring leads and helped Rosie to set up scveral large infusions. 'We'll use O negative blood until we get the cross match result.'

'Any chance of getting him straight to Theatre?'

'Other injuries?'

'Not on a cursory check.'

'We'll do our best—wheel him through.'

The remainder of the surgical team were gradually arriving, so Max and Jenny helped to take their patient up to the emergency theatre suite.

When they eventually left him in the hands of the surgeons, Max said, 'That was hairy.'

'Do you think he'll survive?'

'Don't know—but not for want of trying.'

She shuddered, and he frowned and slid an arm around her. 'Are you OK?'

She nodded. 'It's just the thought… How did you know what it was?'

'The mass was expansile.'

'Pulsating?'

'No more than that. It was expanding and contracting with the heartbeat. Remember that. Not every doctor has seen one.'

Leanne had remained behind to clear up, and when Jenny and Max joined her Max told them, 'You two should be long gone from here. Off you go. Now.'

Jenny gave a tired smile and said, 'We're just going.'

'I'll let you know later how it goes,' he told Jenny as she collected her bits and pieces from the office. 'Would you like me to bring in a takeaway?'

'No. Thanks,' she added belatedly. 'Mum always prepares a meal, so I'll ring once it's cleared away.'

Max was left wondering who else the meal was for—had that stopped her inviting him to join them? As she would have done when they were at Rexford? But then, nothing was the same any more, and he was determined to find out why that very evening.

Although exhausted, Jenny spent an hour with her son before getting him to bed, and so ate later than usual.

'I'm ringing Max later,' she told her mother over their meal, 'and he's coming round for a chat.'

'Why didn't you ask him for a meal? There would have been plenty.'

'It's not a social meeting, Mum. I think he could intend to take Jamie away from me.'

'Why should he want to do that?'

'Look, I can't be sure, but there is a possibility that his fiancée can't have children because she had chemotherapy. We could face losing Jamie, Mum. That's why our chat needs to be businesslike.'

'I see. Well, you won't hear a peep from me. I promise.'

Jenny could tell her mother was disappointed. She'd obviously hoped for a happy ending to their meeting and she wasn't going to get it. Jenny wrapped her arms around her and said, 'Don't worry, Mum. We'll be fine.'

'Right. I'll make myself scarce, then.'

Jenny watched her disappear into the granny flat, aware that she was longing to ask more questions. She hoped she'd have the answers by the end of the evening. She dialled Max's number, and when he answered told him tersely, 'You can come round now. Do you know where I live?'

'I checked before I left the hospital. See you soon.'

Jenny switched the kettle on and placed a bottle of white wine in the fridge just to fill the uneasy time until he arrived.

When he came, she let him in and they stood awkwardly in the hall.

'Coffee?'

He spoke at the same time. 'Thanks for the call.'

They both laughed, but it was strained.

Max said, 'You first.'

'I offered coffee. Or a glass of wine?'

'Coffee is fine, thanks.'

He followed her into the kitchen and she sensed he was looking around her home with interest. 'Nice place.'

'Thanks.'

'Comfortable.'

She nodded as she poured boiling water onto the coffee grounds and placed the cafetière on the tray with two mugs.

He carried the tray through to the living room for her, and placed it on the small table she indicated.

'How did the aneurysm op go?'

'Not well, I'm afraid. I didn't think he stood much of

a chance, but we had to try. On a more cheerful note—remember that young lad who was found with hypothermia this morning?'

'Yes?'

'He's regained consciousness and they've moved him out of ITU already. The resilience of youth.'

'Didn't he have a head injury?'

'Apparently not life-threatening.'

'Was he attacked?'

'I don't think we'll ever know. His parents are swearing never to let him out in the evening again.'

Jenny laughed, but neither of them spoke again until the coffee was poured and they were both seated. Then Max looked around as he had done in the kitchen and said, 'Just the two of us?'

'Apart from Jamie and he's asleep.' What had he expected?

'Your mother lives nearby?'

'In a granny flat. Attached but separate.'

'No one else? No ''lodgers''?'

'Look, Max, what is this about?'

He shrugged. 'Life can't be easy on your salary.'

Recognising his reason for asking, she said, 'It's my mother's house. Now. Can we talk about Jamie, please?'

Max groaned to himself at being caught on the wrong foot. Why on earth had he tried to satisfy his curiosity about who might be paying the mortgage? 'I'd like to meet him, Jenny. And I'm happy to go along with whatever you suggest.'

'Mmm. Do you intend to fight me for custody?'

He stared at her in astonishment. 'That's the last thing I'd thought of.'

'Do you mean that?'

'Of course I mean it. He's my son. He's three years old. And I've never even spoken to him. Surely you can understand how I feel?' Damn. He was allowing himself to get annoyed again, and that was the last thing he'd intended.

'It's your right to meet him, of course. But I'd rather he met you first without knowing who you are. It's bound to come as a shock to him.'

'Like it did for me,' he couldn't prevent himself muttering.

'So you know how he'll feel if you just blurt it out on your first meeting. As you said, he's only three and wouldn't cope.'

'I think you probably underestimate the resilience of children.'

'Max! We're not in A & E now.'

He saw her temper was about to bubble over again and placed a calming hand on her arm. 'Jenny, please. I was about to add that I don't know Jamie, and I'm willing to bow to your wishes for the time being. But I give you fair warning. I want him to know who I am sooner rather than later.'

She sighed and nodded. 'Fair enough. Just let's take it slowly.'

'I'm happy to agree with that. As I said earlier, I won't do anything to deliberately hurt either of you.'

She slid her arm from under his hand. 'Perhaps we could meet in the park some time. Soon.'

'We're both on duty all week, so how about Saturday?'

'I'm afraid not. We're going on holiday that day.'

'Isn't that a conveniently sudden decision? It's not marked down on the staff roster.'

'Actually, it was arranged last week.'

'Where are you going?'

'Majorca.'

'If I can get some time off I could join you for a few days. That would be the ideal time to get to know him.'

'No.' Jenny's objection was vehement. That would be pushing her emotions too far!

'You're not going alone, then?'

'No. Mum is coming with us.'

'Us?'

'Jamie and me.' She frowned at his unexpected query. 'Who did you think I meant?'

'I don't know, Jenny. I don't know anything about your life these days. I was hoping to find out this evening.'

'I don't know what you're suggesting, Max, but my life these days consists of work and looking after Jamie. Nothing more.'

Hope flickered in his heart. He had to know the truth. 'But you left Rexford to live with someone? Someone Jamie thinks of as his father?'

She shook her head. 'There was never anyone else.'

He leaned forward and, resting both his hands on her shoulders started to laugh. 'Oh, Jenny, you have no idea what hearing you say that means to me. I came to Catonbury hoping to find you and see if there was a chance that we might restart our relationship. But when I though you were involved with someone else I backed off straight away.'

'And just as quickly transferred your affections,' she retorted.

'What do you mean?'

'I'm not blind, Max. I know what's going on between you and Rosie.'

'You don't, Jenny. You certainly don't. Our association is purely platonic.'

'Hah! Like your relationship with Clare? You seem to have a lot of those! I have to admit I was surprised to discover you weren't married to Clare already—or did you change your mind when you thought she couldn't have your children?'

Max was stunned into silence by her scathing attack, and before he could gather his wits she pressed it home, 'Is that why you want Jamie? So you can marry Clare and still be a father?'

'Jenny! You don't know what you're saying. You've got it all wrong. I told you. Clare was—is just a friend.'

'Oh, I remember that well. But it wasn't the truth, was it? I was a useful diversion while you were working away from her. Like Rosie is now.'

'No. That's not true, Jenny. Believe me.'

'Well, Clare didn't believe it—and neither did I after I'd spoken to your mother.'

'My mother?'

'Does Rosie know you're just amusing yourself with her while you're at Catonbury. Or—'

'As it happens, she does.' He grasped the top of her arms, as if to emphasise his words. 'And she is doing the same.'

'Huh.' Jenny wriggled her arms free, but he pulled her to him and caught her lips with his own. When he eventually released her, several moments later, he said, 'Doesn't that convince you?'

'It worked once, Max, but no longer.'

'And if I tell you Clare is getting married in three weeks' time to a naval officer you wouldn't believe me, either?'

Jenny stared at him in horror. Was that why he had bothered to look for her so long after their brief affair? Clare was his first choice but she didn't want him any more? So he'd come to look for second best. Recalling his reaction when she'd told him he was a father, she knew he'd found more than he'd bargained for.

Although she hadn't thought it possible, Jenny felt her heart plummet even deeper into her chest. He didn't feel the way she felt about him and never had, and she would probably never have seen him again if things had worked out with Clare. She shook her head miserably. 'I'm sorry, Max. I'm a different person now. You are four years too late. I'll introduce you to Jamie because I know it's your legal right. I'll even arrange for you to see him on a regular basis. But I want nothing more from you. Nothing at all. Do you understand?'

He released her and sank back into his chair, his head buried in his hands. This wasn't how he'd envisaged the evening going at all. He still wasn't sure how it had come about, but it was no longer important. Jenny believed he had two-timed her—was *still* two-timing her—and had been badly hurt. No words were ever going to persuade her of his sincerity, that he loved her and wanted nothing more than to spend the rest of his life taking care of her and their son. It was going to take much, much more than a flowery speech if he was going to convince her it was all a mistake. He would have to prove it to her by his actions and it wasn't going to happen overnight.

If only he hadn't been so quick to believe she wanted nothing more to do with him. He moved to the settee alongside her and slid a gentle arm around her. 'I don't want to fight with you, Jenny. Can we at least be friends and work this out in a civilised way? It's obvious I hurt you in the past, and I certainly don't want to do so ever again.'

He saw she was struggling to keep back tears and he

wiped a stray one from her cheek with his thumb. 'The past three years haven't been easy for you, have they?'

She tried to smile. 'I've been lucky. A home and child-care there for the asking...'

But not the thing you wanted most, he thought miserably. A normal family life with Jamie's father. He *had* to convince her that was what he wanted, too.

'Can I get you another coffee?' he asked gently.

She shook her head. 'No, thanks, or I'll never sleep.' She turned her head and met his eyes. 'If we *could* handle this in a friendly way it would be so much better for Jamie.'

He wanted to rage and shout—Just for Jamie? What about us? But he resisted the temptation. The most lasting relationships were supposed be based on friendship, so he would have to be patient.

'That's fine by me.' He grasped her hands tightly between his own and, looking closely into her eyes, said, 'Friends? Agreed?'

She nodded. 'Agreed.'

Neither spoke again for several moments, but their eyes remained locked. Eventually he could resist it no longer and hugged her to him before kissing her gently.

She didn't object, so he deepened the kiss, but this time she pushed him away. 'Friends. Remember?'

His answer was a wry grin.

'About your meeting with Jamie, Max. As we're both working for the rest of the week it looks as if it's going to have to wait until we get back from holiday.'

'No. I've had a better idea.' Desperation was making his brain work overtime.

'What's that?'

'How are you getting to the airport?'

'I'll take the car and leave it in the car park.'

'I'll take you there. And collect you. Save the parking charges.'

'But—'

'You can tell Jamie someone from work has offered to take you. What could be more natural? At least I'll get to know him a little before you leave the country, and he'll be so excited he won't wonder about me.'

After a moment's thought, she said slowly. 'I suppose it might work…'

'But?'

'It means explaining to Mum, which won't be easy.'

'Of course,' he joked tentatively. 'She thinks I'm a threat to Jamie.'

Jenny laughed. 'Not any longer. She thinks Jamie ought to know who you are.'

He was suddenly serious. 'Tell her he will. When the time is right.'

CHAPTER EIGHT

HE REALLY meant it! He wasn't fighting her any more. Jenny felt a huge wave of relief sweep through her as she impulsively hugged him. 'Thanks for saying that, Max. I know it's not easy for you, but I really do think this is the right way.'

'I know, love, and whatever you may think I only want what's best for all of us.'

'I realise that now we've had this chat.' She yawned, feeling able to relax for the first time in weeks.

He checked his watch. 'I'd no idea it was so late. I must be off.'

Suddenly reluctant to let him go, she offered, 'A night-cap? Or another coffee?'

Aware that if he stayed he was in danger of overstepping the boundaries of friendship, he shook his head. 'Not tonight, thanks.'

She saw him to the door. 'Thank you again, Max, for being so reasonable.'

'You and me both.' He slid his arms round her and kissed her lightly. 'Goodnight, Jenny.'

This time she didn't try to escape, but rested her head on his chest until the familiar maleness of him and the feel of his heart beating against her ear caused such a surge of longing to spread through her that she pulled away, trembling and confused.

'See you tomorrow,' he all but whispered, and let himself out, leaving her to make her way slowly back to the living room, wishing things were still as they had been in the heady days of their first meeting.

Her mother knocked on the adjoining door, and when Jenny didn't answer called, 'Are you OK, Jenny?'

'Fine, Mum. Just off to bed.' The last thing she needed at that moment was to chat. She wanted to savour a little longer the feel of his arms around her and the scent of him in her nostrils. Her mother took the hint, and after saying goodnight left her alone.

For the first time since Max had reappeared on the scene she awoke feeling refreshed. Although her dreams had been of Max, they'd been of their time together at Rexford and she had enjoyed every minute of them.

'How did it go last night?' her mother asked over breakfast.

'Fine. I think we both know where we stand.'

'So you're going to tell Jamie who he is?'

'Not before our holiday.'

'But that's—'

Before she could voice her opinion, Jenny interrupted, 'Max has offered to run us to the airport. Jamie will get to know him then, as a colleague from work. It's what we both agreed is best, Mum,' she told her gently, indicating the matter was closed.

'I suppose I'll have to go along with it, then.'

'Yes, Mum, you will. Don't forget you'll be meeting him properly for the first time as well!'

The next days passed in a flurry of preparations both at home and at work, until on Friday evening Jenny wondered if going on holiday was really worth it.

Eventually everything was ready and packed, and she sank into bed exhausted—to be woken too soon by the doorbell.

Already dressed, her mother had introduced herself and

invited Max into the hallway by the time Jenny rushed downstairs in the short, short nightdress that Max had once said was his favourite as it came off so easily.

She caught his eye and knew he was remembering, too. 'The cases are ready. I only have to dress myself and Jamie,' she told him hastily.

'I'm a tad early,' he replied, with a grin still lingering on his lips. 'Didn't want you to miss your flight.'

Wishing she'd stopped to put on her dressing gown, she fled back up the stairs and woke Jamie.

After a struggle, she got them both dressed and they made their way downstairs. He didn't even look at Max, but murmured, 'Want breakfast.'

'I've got it in the bag. You can have a picnic at the airport.'

Jamie was satisfied with that, and allowed himself to be carried out and seated in the child seat Max had placed in the car. Within seconds he was sound asleep again.

'What about *your* breakfast?' Max asked on the way to the airport.

'I'll get something on the plane, no doubt.'

He shook his head and told her, 'We'll breakfast in the restaurant after you've checked in.' She was about to protest that there was no need for him to come into the airport when she realised the very reason for his transporting them hadn't even noticed their driver.

There was already a queue at the check-in desk for the Majorca flight, and Max, who had loaded their luggage onto a trolley and sat Jamie on top, indicated she and her mother should stand in line while he moved the trolley with them, just outside the barrier.

An airport announcement woke Jamie, and after rubbing his eyes he looked first at Jenny, then at Max. 'Who're you?'

'I work with your mother. I'm called Max.'

The boy started to wriggle dangerously, so Max lifted him down beside Jenny. Sucking his thumb, he hid himself behind her leg.

She raised her eyebrows apologetically.

'Give him time to wake up,' Max murmured as he pushed the trolley forward. He smiled at Mrs Stalham. 'I think we'll all feel better when we've had some breakfast.'

'I've had mine,' she told him.

'Cup of coffee, then?'

'Now you're talking.'

Jenny watched the exchange and saw that her mother was already succumbing to his charm.

Once they were checked in, Max returned the luggage trolley to the rack and indicated the restaurant. Jamie protested. 'Wanna ride on the trolley.'

'We don't need it any more. You can walk,' his mother told him.

He sat down on the floor with his thumb back in his mouth and nothing Jenny said would make him move. Embarrassed, she was about to drag him to his feet when Max bent down and whispered, 'Do you want a piggyback?'

Jamie leapt to his feet and clambered onto Max's shoulders.

When they arrived at the restaurant Audrey Stalham found an empty table and suggested Jamie stayed there with her while Max and Jenny collected some food and drink.

There was no way he was going to climb down off Max's shoulders until Jenny produced a small size pack of his favourite cereal and a mug full of milk.

'Nice lad,' he complimented as they joined a small queue.

'I'm warning you here and now, Dr Field,' she teased, 'if you are going to spoil him in this way I'll have second thoughts about your access to him.'

'In that case,' he retorted, 'no breakfast for you.'

'Too late.' She was smiling happily as she helped herself to a round of toast.

'Oh, it is good to see the old Jenny again.'

'Hey. Not so much of the old, thank you.'

'The young and full of fun one, then. I do wish I was coming to Majorca with you.'

'Someone has to keep the department going.'

He didn't look as if he relished the task.

'It's only a week. You'll be back at the airport to collect us before you know it.'

'Can't wait,' he told her over his shoulder as he paid at the cash desk.

They carried their trays over to the table and ate their breakfast in a companionable silence. Mrs Stalham soon made up for it, asking Max about his job and his family.

To Jenny's relief, when she started to veer towards dangerous topics Jamie finished his breakfast and climbed down to stand between Max and Jenny. He'd gradually accepted Max and now began to answer his questions.

At the end of a serious discussion on aeroplanes, Jenny indicated they should go through to the departure lounge. Max agreed and said to Jamie, 'Would you like me to collect you when you come home? Or are you going to walk?'

Jamie's eyes slid to his mother and she answered. 'As we have all those cases, I think we'd like you to come back for us—don't you, Jamie?'

He nodded enthusiastically. 'Yes, please.'

Max grasped both of her arms tightly and dropped a casual kiss on her lips. 'Have a good holiday, love. You deserve it.' Unable to help himself, he enveloped her in a bear hug. 'I'm going to miss you,' he whispered in her ear. 'Come back safely.'

Jenny returned his kiss and reluctantly made her way up to the security barrier.

Clearly delighted by their rapport, Audrey thanked him as well, and shook his hand warmly.

In spite of the improvement in their relationship, it was a relief to get away. Jenny settled back into her seat and watched as the aircraft lifted rapidly from the ground. A whole week in which she could take stock and recharge her batteries.

'Why isn't Max coming with us?'

Jenny was used to Jamie's never-ending questions, but this one surprised her.

'He's far too busy at the hospital. I won't be there, will I?'

'I want him to come.' He pursed his lips in a determined sulk, making Jenny turn to her mother with a happy smile.

'There he is. W-waving.' Jamie was so eager to convince her that he really could see him that he stumbled over the word.

'Waving? At us?'

'I told you, Mummy. Didn't you hear me?'

Suppressing a smile at him copying her own admonishment, used when he pretended not hear it was bedtime, she nodded and gave him a hug.

'Can he come with us next time?'

'Perhaps. Lean over me and look down there.' Jenny pointed out the fast-receding land and Jamie promptly forgot all about him.

She tipped her seat back and closed her eyes, and tried not to think about Max. He refused to be banished from her thoughts. For once she was actually grateful when Jamie's questions began again and she could put to the back of her mind the problems that she still had to face on her return.

Their holiday package included a car, and once the travel rep at the airport had sorted out her paperwork Jenny loaded their cases into the boot and set off for the north coast, where their apartment for the week was located.

Her mother sat in the back with Jamie, who was in the child's car seat provided. Once or twice Jenny checked in the rearview mirror and saw they were both napping. No problem. She had mapped out the route carefully and knew exactly where they were going—which was more than could be said for the driver of the pick-up truck that hurtled from a side street.

In the split second before he hit them Jenny swung the wheel to the left, but couldn't avoid the impact. The truck ploughed into the front passenger side of the car.

Jenny was vaguely aware that the resultant jolt had woken her mother and Jamie, who had started screaming, but when she tried to rouse herself to comfort them she couldn't. A strange lethargy had invaded her head when it hit the driver's door. She closed her eyes and the next thing she knew her mother was trying to tell someone she had been knocked out.

Her mother's voice made her think about Jamie. She attempted to struggle up and say she was OK, but couldn't as she was held by a firm pair of hands.

'Where—Jamie? Where's Jamie?'

'Your son?' a masculine voice asked. 'He's OK. With my colleague.' Jenny tried to turn her head and see him, but found she was prevented from doing so by something rigid around her neck.

'Do you hurt anywhere else?'

Jenny took quite a few seconds to think about the question and eventually tried to shake her head. 'My head aches. And this hurts my neck.' She pulled at the collar.

Her hand was gently restrained. She saw with relief it was her mother's hand, and said urgently, 'Jamie—is he with you?'

'He's fine. He wasn't hurt at all. Just a bit frightened.'

'Hurt?' she queried. 'What happened?'

'A small lorry hit the car and you banged your head. Jamie and I were fine in the back.'

'So what—?'

It was the male voice that replied. 'You are in Majorca, Senora. In hospital. Now I need to check out if you are hurt anywhere.'

As he did so she realised he was doing the kind of check they would do in her own department and asked her mother, 'Is this casualty?'

Her mother nodded.

'How did I get here?'

'The police called an ambulance.'

'Why?' She frowned.

'You banged your head when the truck hit our car. We were on our way to the apartment. Remember?'

Jenny struggled to, but it was like trying to dredge up facts through a stringy fog. 'I don't remember the apartment.'

'We didn't get that far.'

'Try not to worry. Your holiday rep is on the way,' the male voice reassured her. 'She'll sort it.'

I want to see Jamie. Now.' She was suddenly terrified

that he was badly injured—or worse—and they were keeping him away from her.

'You fetch him?' the man she now presumed was a doctor asked her mother.

She nodded, and was back moments later with Jamie in her arms. 'There's Mummy, Jamie, but she's very tired. Give her a quick kiss and then we'll let her rest.'

'Why's she crying?' he asked, as tears streamed down her cheeks.

'She's pleased to see you.'

'What's that on her neck?'

'It stops her moving her head.'

'Why?'

'Because she banged it.'

'I don't have one of those when I bang my head,' he complained.

Jenny pulled him to her chest. 'This was a big bang, so the doctor is being careful. That's all.'

He looked round him suspiciously. To everyone's relief the representative of the holiday firm arrived at that moment, and as well as diverting Jamie's attention took control of everything.

Some time later, after another extensive check of Jenny's condition, the doctor removed the collar from her neck and conversed in Spanish with the rep.

She told Jenny, 'It looks as if you'll be able to leave here soon. He says you are concussed and need rest, but you should be all right if there's someone to keep an eye on you. As you're the driver in your party I think we ought to take you all back to a hotel for the night, where help is available if necessary. I'll pick up your luggage and sort things out with the police.'

Jenny nodded and immediately regretted the movement as it made her feel nauseous.

To her relief, the sickness soon settled, and she was able to gradually raise herself to a sitting position without too much of a traumatic effect.

The doctor handed the rep a sheet of instructions.

'He wants you to read these carefully in case you need further attention. I'll translate them for you.'

Jenny managed a weak grin. 'I work in an accident and emergency department in England. I know what to look out for.'

Jenny was fine, and the next morning, the rep moved them to their apartment and offered to find another car for them.

The beach was within five minutes' walking distance, so Jenny said, 'I can't say I feel much like driving yet. I think we'll manage without—apart from getting to the airport next Sunday.'

'I can arrange for a transfer. Any extra expense you'll have to sort out with your insurance company.'

Jenny nodded ruefully. 'I'll do all that when we get home. I don't fancy concentrating on paperwork at the moment.'

For the remainder of the week Jenny had a permanent headache, and she felt tired and dispirited. They took it very easy—Jenny often sleeping while her mother entertained Jamie on the beach. She felt bad about that, but couldn't raise the energy to do anything about it.

'I'm sorry, Mum. This hasn't been anything of a holiday for you,' she told her while they were waiting at the airport.

'You don't look any better for it, either. You've looked so strained over the past few weeks I was hoping this would have done you a lot of good. That truck driver has a lot to answer for.'

Close to tears, Jenny nodded carefully. Her head still ached and she wanted desperately to lie down and sleep.

When they arrived back in England, she took one look at the luggage conveyor belt and burst into tears.

'I don't think I can manage it, Mum. Not yet,' she sobbed. 'I'll get a trolley in a moment.' She sniffed and tried to gain control, but she was emotionally exhausted.

'Go and sit over there,' her mother instructed. 'I'll bring the luggage over when it appears, and then find some help if we need it.'

'Leave Jamie with me.'

'If you're sure.'

It seemed a long time before her mother returned, and when she did she was smiling. Jamie was sitting quietly looking at the pictures in a travel brochure and Jenny was feeling a little better.

'Someone'll be here before long,' her mother told her.

Jenny nodded her thanks. 'I'm sorry for being such a wimp.'

'You're not.'

'Hello, Jenny.' Max was standing before them.

'How—how did you get in here?'

'Your mother pulled a few strings.'

'Mu-um, you didn't— How did you manage that?'

'I told Customs you'd had an accident and were feeling ill. I said a doctor was collecting us and they assumed he was someone organised by the insurance company.'

'But you don't even know his surname.'

'They asked over the PA system for the doctor who had come to collect you.'

'You shouldn't have done that, Mum.'

While they were arguing Max quietly loaded the cases onto the back of a motorised buggy and told Jamie and her mother to climb in.

Jenny remained seated where she was.

'Come on, Jenny. Do you need a hand?' Max took her arm.

She shuddered at his touch and he looked at her closely. 'Are you all right?'

She nodded. 'I'm fine.'

'Well, you certainly don't look it. Come on. Let's get you home.'

Jenny allowed herself to be helped into the seat beside her mother. He looked down at her and then towards her mother and shook his head. 'Thank goodness you're home, where I can keep an eye on her. She's doesn't seem to be at all well.'

'Talk *to* me. Not about me,' Jenny muttered. 'I'm fine. It was just a shock.'

Max raised his eyebrows and strode round to sit beside the driver.

They soon arrived at his car, where he assisted Jenny's transfer to the passenger seat. He pulled the belt and leaned across her to fasten it before helping her mother and Jamie into the back.

When he arrived at their front door Max leapt out and released Jamie from his car seat. Taking his hand, he waited until Mrs Stalham came round and took the boy inside. Then he went to help Jenny from the car, but before he did so he leaned into the car and kissed her lightly. 'Do you want me to stay?'

She shrank away from him. 'Certainly not. Thank you for rescuing us. I'm sorry to have caused you so much trouble. I don't know how she found you.'

'It was no trouble—'

'She shouldn't have done it.'

'Why not? It was my son who needed the transport.'

'Is that what she said?'

'That's privileged information, but I should say she was more worried about you.' He helped her from the car.

She shrugged her arm free. 'You should be at work.'

He frowned and looked at her quizzically. 'I'm off duty today. I told you so last week. If you like I'll look after Jamie for a while.'

She looked at him with narrowed eyes. 'Jamie's staying with me,' she ground out through her teeth. 'He doesn't know you.'

'Of course he does.' She didn't actually call him stupid, but it was tempting. Very tempting—especially when he answered, 'He remembers the piggyback I gave him.'

'Piggyback? I don't know what you're talking about.' She gave a dismissive wave of her hand. 'Thank you. See you around.'

'I'm not leaving you until I'm sure you're all right.'

She heaved an exasperated sigh. 'I told you, there's nothing wrong with me.'

'OK. I'll carry your luggage in.'

He placed the cases in the hallway and followed her through to the kitchen. 'Would you like some tea?' Audrey Stalham asked.

'That's be great. Do you need milk, or anything else from the supermarket?'

'The milkman left us some, thanks, and we've plenty of food in the freezer.'

Jenny watched him suspiciously, and when Jamie clambered up onto Max's knee she ordered sharply, 'Get down at once.'

Jamie was obviously upset, and Max cuddled him before letting him go, despite Jenny's glare.

Max turned to Mrs Stalham and asked, 'Are Jamie's toys next door?' He indicated the living room with his head.

Mrs Stalham was quick to take the hint. 'I'll take him through to find them.'

Max pulled his chair up in front of Jenny and took both her hands in his. 'What's wrong, Jenny? Is it your head?'

She snatched her hands away and didn't speak.

'Can you remember the accident?'

'A truck hit my car and I banged my head.'

'What colour truck?'

'Does it matter whether it was red, blue or green? All I know is it ruined my holiday.'

'It matters,' he told her gently, 'because I don't think you remember the actual moment of impact, just what you have been told.'

'So?'

'I think you were concussed, and you still need rest. Your head *does* ache, doesn't it?'

She nodded reluctantly. 'But it's getting better. I'll be fine for work on Monday.'

'I think not. Who's your GP?'

'Why?'

'Don't you really remember me giving Jamie a piggyback at the airport?'

She thought hard, then nodded. 'Yes. I do.'

'Thank goodness for that. If you hadn't I was going to insist you came straight in to see the neurologist.'

She frowned. 'Why?'

'How far back you've forgotten things that have happened is an indication of the severity of your head injury. Do you remember driving the car you hired?'

She nodded carefully.

'That's something, at least, but I still think you should rest—and you need looking after.'

'Mum's here.'

'She'll have enough with Jamie to contend with.'

Jenny tried to think but her brain wouldn't co-operate. 'I'm just tired after the journey. I'll be all right after an early night.'

'I'll ring tomorrow to see how you are.' He leant forward and kissed her on the forehead. 'If you feel OK then perhaps I could come round—'

Jenny panicked. 'There's no need, thanks. We'll be fine.'

'But I want to spend some time with you all.'

'We'll talk about it again when I feel better.'

He shook his head. 'Take care of yourself, Jenny. I'll tell your mother I'm off.'

It was some time later when she heard the front door bang, and she knew they'd probably been discussing her.

She made her way through to find her mother.

'How are you feeling now, dear?'

'Better. I just needed the rest. I'll see to Jamie and give you a break.'

'He's very caring, isn't he?'

'Max? Yes, he's a good doctor.'

'He cares a lot about you as well.'

'If you say so.'

'Don't you think so?'

'He cares about everybody.'

Her mother had to be satisfied with that, but Jenny knew she wouldn't rest until she discovered why her daughter was keeping such an eligible bachelor at bay. Especially when he was her child's father.

Max was not happy. It seemed to him Jenny was using her head injury to conveniently forget the decisions they'd come to about Jamie. He knew she probably had post-concussional syndrome, and needed time, but his son was growing up every day and he wanted him to know he was his father as soon as possible.

He'd spoken to her mother soon after breakfast, but Jenny hadn't wanted to speak to him on the phone. When he'd suggested he go round there later she'd asked her mother to say she was taking the day quietly, as he'd suggested.

She was apparently still insisting she would be back at work on Monday morning and she wanted to rest. So did he, but he was too agitated to do so.

In the end he went into work after a scratch lunch from his refrigerator. Great weekend this was turning out to be, after his high hopes for a relationship with Jenny and Jamie. It was a cruel setback when everything had been going so well between them before she'd left for Majorca.

All he could do was make sure his paperwork was up to date for when she returned the next day.

'Haven't you got a home to go to, Max?' Rosie asked him when she had a lull between patients.

'Doesn't look like it, does it?'

'I thought you were picking Jenny up from the airport.'

'That was yesterday. She was in a car crash out there, and is resting quietly today.'——

'Was she hurt?'

'She had a head injury. Concussion. They didn't keep her in the hospital, but she's not right.'

Rosie perched on the corner of his desk. 'When did it happen?'

'The day they arrived, apparently.'

'That's a week. How is it affecting her?'

'Headache. Lethargy. Still a bit of memory loss. Irritability where I'm concerned!'

'Poor old you. Do you think she needs a check X-ray?'

'I don't think so. I checked her pupils and pulse without

her realising it. These things take time, as you well know. I tried to persuade her not to come back to work tomorrow, because I don't think she'll find it easy to cope with a full day, but I think I'm the last person she's prepared to listen to at the moment.'

'Poor Max. Just when you thought things were on the up between you. Do you want to come over for a meal later?'

'I don't think so. Thanks all the same, Rosie.'

'OK. I'll have a chat with Jenny tomorrow and see what I can do.'

'Don't do that, for goodness' sake. She has no idea you know anything about us.'

'Keep your hair on, Max. I was only going to chat about her head injury. You said she wouldn't listen to what you had to say.'

He grinned. 'That's my girl.'

'You'd better not let Jenny hear you say that or you *will* be out in the cold. Permanently.'

Jenny struggled out of bed, reluctant to get up at such an unearthly hour. Why hadn't she taken Max's advice and taken some time off sick?

She dressed and crept down the stairs without waking Jamie. 'Can I leave him to you today, Mum?' she asked when her mother joined her for breakfast.

'No problem. But are you sure you're fit to go to work?'

'Stop fussing. You're as bad as Max, Mum,' she told her irritably.

'Perhaps because we both care about you—'

'Don't let him fool you. All Max cares about is Jamie.'

Audrey Stalham frowned. 'He certainly didn't give *me*

that impression. And neither did you when he took us to the airport. I haven't seen you so happy for a long time.'

'He's a con man, Mum. He could charm sheep into laying eggs if he wanted to. I know. I've been taken in by him before and nearly was again last week. It took that knock on my head to bring me to my senses.'

'He's Jamie's father. You can't deny him contact with the lad.'

'No. But I can deny him everything else. Can't I?'

CHAPTER NINE

JENNY found it a struggle to motivate herself once she arrived at work, especially when she saw the packed waiting area.

To make matters worse, halfway through the hectic morning the hospital's internal investigators came in search of Max to ask more questions about the stabbed youth who had died. They also wanted to interview all the other members of staff who had been on duty that day.

When her turn came Jenny was fiercely defensive of Max, acclaiming his superior skills as a doctor as well as emphasising what a caring person he was. In every way.

'I think we've got the picture, Sister.' The investigator grinned. 'All we need now is to speak to him again.'

'He's tied up in the resuscitation room.'

'We'll just wait in here, then. Perhaps you'd let him know?'

'He's far too busy to waste time answering questions,' she snapped, annoyed they were refusing to leave.

'It's only a few routine questions—we won't keep him long, I promise.'

'Have you seen the waiting room?'

'We're prepared to wait, Sister.'

Eventually Max joined them in the office, and before she left Jenny warned them again that he could only spare a moment.

She joined Rosie and Lisa in the resuscitation room. 'I'll take over here if you want a break, Lisa.'

'Why don't you both stay?' Rosie asked quickly. 'We could do with an another pair of hands.'

When they had eventually made some inroads into the number of patients waiting Jenny sent as many of her staff for their lunch break as she could.

'Why don't you go home for the rest of the day, Jenny?' Rosie suggested. 'That knock on your head hasn't done you any favours.'

'I do feel a bit washed out, but I'll be OK when I've had some lunch. I could have done without the investigation this morning.'

As she worked on Jenny felt Max was wanting to say something to her, but he controlled himself and confined what he had to say to information about the patients.

However, when Jenny had slipped into the office to collect money for her lunch, he came in behind her and said, 'Jenny?'

'Yes?' she asked apprehensively, aware he'd been brooding over whatever he was going to say.

'The allegations about that boy's death haven't been proved. They're going to close the case.'

Relief made her blurt out, 'Thank goodness for that.'

'So you don't have to tell lies about me any more.' He chuckled. 'Don't think I don't appreciate it, but if you'd continued to defend me so hotly they might have had second thoughts. They already think you're protesting my innocence too much.'

Unable to recognise his teasing when she was already having difficulty in coping with the work, she glared at him balefully then, without a word, spun on her heel and stalked out of the office. The slam of the door resounded through the department.

Rosie, who had been coming to see if they were able to take a break, sped off in pursuit. 'Lunchtime, Jenny.'

She took her arm and led her down to the canteen. 'What can I get you?'

Jenny didn't answer, but looked vaguely at the selection of food.

'Vegetable lasagne OK?'

Jenny nodded and fumbled in her pocket for money she knew wasn't there.

'My treat,' said Rosie. 'Grab that table in the corner, then we can be private.'

When Rosie had set the food in front of her, she thanked her but made no attempt to eat.

'Jenny, I'm worried about you. You're not well. You need a few more quiet days to recover.'

The tears that Jenny had been damming back spilled over, and she pushed back her chair and fled from the interested gaze of those around her.

Max, who had just arrived in the canteen in search of her, followed after indicating to Rosie she should finish her meal.

He found Jenny on a bench behind the outpatient department.

'I'm taking you home. Now.'

'I'm all right.' She sniffed, trying desperately to compose herself.

He grinned and gently smoothed back the hair from her forehead. 'You look it.'

She tried to glare at him and failed miserably. 'I don't know what's the matter with me.'

'As the most experienced accident and emergency nurse in the department you ought to!'

She looked startled.

'How often have you told patients with concussion not

to go back to work too soon and to try not to do too much?'

'It's over a week—'

'So?'

'I haven't done much.'

'Except struggle back from Majorca after an accident with all your luggage and a three-year-old child, and then come into work in the busiest, most pressurised department in the hospital. Not to mention the emotional strain of me trying to get my hands on Jamie. Not that I am,' he told her hurriedly. 'But that's what you still think, isn't it?'

'I don't know what to think any more.'

'Jenny,' he told her softly, 'you didn't wait long enough earlier to hear all I was about to say. You see, I was very heartened this morning to discover that you trust me sufficiently to defend me the way you did.'

When she looked up at him he was pleased to see some of her usual fighting spirit returning to her eyes. 'I was talking about your work. Nothing else.'

A wry smile tugged at his lips. 'Why am I not surprised? Come on.' He took her arm and gently raised her to feet. 'I'll take you to the changing room, then have a word with Rosie. She'll hold the fort until I get back.'

His touch on her arm set off a tremble that spread rapidly through her body. Noting it, he moved his arm protectively round her shoulders and turned her to face him. 'Not only will I never hurt either of you, Jenny, I'd like to do my damnedest to make your lives comfortable and happy,' he told her softly. 'But I can only do it if you trust me.'

'I—'

'At the moment I don't know where I stand with you. I want to take care of you, Jenny. It sure as hell breaks my heart when I see you like this and I'm not able to do a damn thing about it. But the last thing I'm going to do is rush you. And stop worrying about Jamie. I'm prepared to wait. I'll take you home now and run your car back later. Rosie'll pick me up, I'm sure. Then I won't bother you any more. If you want me, you know where to contact me.'

His words brought forth a fresh storm of weeping and she sagged forward with her head on his chest. He wrapped his arms around her and rocked her gently to and fro.

'I'm sorry. I can't think straight at the moment, Max,' she sobbed out. 'I wish I'd never gone on that damned holiday.'

'I work in Accident and Emergency as well, don't forget, and I understand. Just get yourself better and then we'll talk.' With that he frogmarched her to the changing room.

When they arrived at her front door, he asked, 'Got your keys?'

She handed them to him.

He opened the front door and then stood back to let her go in.

'See you when you're better, Jen.' He bent forward and brushed her lips with the softest of kisses. 'Make it soon.'

He wanted to sweep her into his arms and up into bed, as he had done the night Jamie was conceived, but he was sure it would be the worst thing he could do in the present situation. So he turned and walked back to the car.

Jenny watched him drive away and closed the door, unaware that her mother was standing behind her.

'What are you doing home at this time?'

'Max said I wasn't fit enough to be there.'

'I can't say I blame him. Your pallor is enough to frighten the patients away. Why didn't you ask him in?'

'He had to get back to work. Can I get through and sit down, Mum? I feel quite shaky.'

'I'm not surprised after that kiss.' She led the way into the living room.

Jenny's cheeks coloured. 'You saw it?'

'Yep. And if you try to tell me again that guy doesn't love you, I won't believe it. Whatever may have happened in the past.'

Jenny shrugged. 'We'll see.'

'Why don't you go to bed for an hour or two?'

'It would scare Jamie if he found me there.'

'He won't be home from nursery for another hour.'

'I think I will, then.' Anything to get away from her mother's inquisition.

With rest, Jenny's condition improved rapidly, and on Friday she knew she was nearly back to normal and would be fit for work on Monday. But for the first time she could remember she didn't want to go.

She hadn't heard from Max since he'd deposited her on the doorstep. He had left her car on the drive and posted the keys through the letterbox without a word.

Rosie had rung nearly every day to check on her progress, so she guessed he was getting a regular bulletin. His silence hurt, but she guessed it was partly her own fault.

She'd not been very nice to him on her return from Majorca, and she must have seemed ungrateful for his help both that day and on Monday.

Her mood wasn't helped by Jamie repeatedly asking when they could see him again. 'I just don't know until

I see him at work on Monday, love,' she told him after he'd mentioned Max again.

'Why don't you ring *him*?' her mother asked later that evening.

Jenny thought about that kiss on the doorstep and his whispered 'Make it soon'.

'I'd rather not, Mum. He'll be in touch when he wants to see Jamie again. I'll see him soon enough.'

Her mother shook her head but wisely decided to say no more.

However, Jenny spent the next couple of hours convincing herself that she ought to ring and offer him the chance to see Jamie the next day. Perhaps in the park.

Once her mother had retired to her own rooms for the night, and Jamie was asleep, she lifted the receiver and dialled Max's number. After four rings the answer machine cut in and she quickly replaced it.

Probably gone home for the weekend, she told herself, unwilling to admit he might be out with Rosie.

She tried the number again on Sunday morning, but with the same result, and she didn't know if she was pleased or sorry.

When she walked into her office on Monday morning there was a floral arrangement on her desk. A light touch had been used to produce a pastel nosegay, not too big or gaudy, with a subtle fragrance.

There was a small card in front of it saying, 'Welcome back'.

'What lovely flowers,' she said to Donna, when she came in to give the hand-over report.

'They are, aren't they? I don't know where they came from.'

'One of the day girls probably brought them in.'

'I don't think so. Leanne asked me if I'd done it.'

'Oh, well. It was nice of somebody. Makes me feel better about coming back already.'

'You're like me. Hate that first day when you've been away.'

'I think everybody does. It's that feeling that you don't know what's been happening in your absence.'

As soon as she could Jenny did a tour of her department, just to make sure that *nothing* had been changed.

Rosie greeted her warmly. 'You look better. Much better. We missed you, but the rest has obviously done you good. Did you like the flowers?'

Jenny felt an absurd disappointment that they were from Rosie, but said, 'They're beautiful. Such delicate colours. Thank you so much for them.'

'Oh, they're not from me,' Rosie exclaimed. 'Max brought them in. On his day off, too.'

'He was on call over the weekend, then?' Jenny said.

'Yep, and they had a right time of it, I think. Apparently he hardly got to bed at all Saturday night.'

Jenny tried to hide her relief that he hadn't been out with Rosie. Or anyone else! 'This place gets worse, doesn't it? And by the looks of that waiting area it's not going to be much better today. We'd better make a start.'

There were so many patients to see that Jenny didn't get back to her office until nearly lunchtime, but when she did she felt such a warmth spread through her at the sight of the flowers that she decided to ring Max immediately and invite him over to the house when she got home from work.

'Thank you for the flowers, Max,' she told him when he answered. 'They're just the kind of colours I like.'

'I know. If you remember you told me once they were the colours you would have in your wedding bouquet.'

And he'd hadn't forgotten! With difficulty she gulped

down the lump in her throat before saying, 'If you're not doing anything, would you like to come over for a cup of tea with Jamie when I get home?'

He appeared to hesitate. 'If you're sure that's what you want, Jen, and that you won't be too tired after your first day back.'

'If you'd seen this place this morning you'd have known I'll be exhausted. But—but I know you've probably missed seeing Jamie.'

'You've no idea how much.'

I can imagine, she thought. Aloud, she said, 'I should be home by five. I'll see you then.'

The afternoon flew by, not giving her a chance to worry about whether she'd done the right thing or not. She was just about to leave when the red phone rang, warning of a multiple pile-up in Darwin Road.

'How many casualties?' she asked Lisa, who hadn't long arrived on duty.

'Four on stretchers. I don't know if there are any more.'

With a sinking heart Jenny knew she couldn't leave until they'd been sorted. Especially with Max not there. She also knew that it was going to take her much longer than usual to get home—until the accident was cleared. Darwin Road was the only road she could take from the hospital.

She tried to ring her mother, but the telephone was engaged and she didn't have another chance as the ambulance with the first casualty was approaching.

She met it with Rosie and Zac, the new senior registrar who had started work while Jenny was away.

With the paramedics' help the casualty was rushed through to the resus room and transferred from the trolley. 'He's called Brett Summers.'

'Get the monitoring leads on, Jenny, and stand by to

shock him if necessary—his last trace doesn't look too good and his blood pressure is dropping. I'll get another line in.'

'Plasma expander, Lisa. Quickly. And blood for cross-matching. Then check X-ray are on their way.'

'Two more casualties just arriving,' Fran, the health care assistant, told Jenny.

'Any details?'

'None except that one is shocked and the other has a whiplash injury.'

Jenny nodded to indicate that she had heard. 'Get the paramedics to wheel them straight through.'

By the time they arrived the first casualty appeared more or less under control, so Jenny joined Zac in looking at the two new arrivals. 'Any more to come?' she asked the paramedics as they were about to leave.

'They're just cutting one out of a BMW.'

'What colour?' Although she knew Max would drive along that road to her house she asked the question automatically, not expecting them to know.

When they said dark green her heart gave an erratic leap of fear. Telling herself there must be hundreds of dark green BMWs around, she tried to push any thought of it from her mind and concentrate on the next two casualties.

But she couldn't help asking questions. 'Did you see the driver?' she asked the nearest paramedic. 'Our new consultant has a dark green one.'

He shook his head. 'Wouldn't know him if I saw him, Sister. And from the state of the car I probably wouldn't recognise him if I did.'

She couldn't prevent a gasp of horror at that answer, and Rosie came over to say quietly, 'It would be a chance in a million.' Then, more loudly for everyone's benefit,

'Brett's condition is not stabilising, so I've asked the surgeons to take a look. He's bleeding somewhere.'

'Another ambulance arriving,' Fran warned them.

Zac and Jenny arrived at the same moment.

'DOA, I'm afraid. Just need a doctor to certify the death.'

What colour was left drained from Jenny's face as Zac pushed her out of the way and climbed into the ambulance. 'Was there anyone with him? Relatives or friends?'

'Nope. He's obviously a rep, judging by the boxes that were stacked up in his car, so I shouldn't think he's from this area.'

It was only a few moments, but it seemed like an hour to Jenny before she processed the news that it wasn't Max. All she had been able to think of was Jamie. If Max had died without Jamie knowing he was his father she would never have forgiven herself. She knew then that she had to tell him, and allow Max to spend as much time with his son as he wanted.

It was after six when she eventually made it home. Max's car was in the drive and she was so pleased to see it that she ran a caressing hand along the bonnet. Letting herself into the house, she heard sounds of merriment coming from the bathroom. Aware that they hadn't heard her above the noise, she crept upstairs to find them.

As Max and her mother both had their backs to her, Jamie was the first to notice her. 'Mummy,' he squealed. 'Max is going to be my dad. He'll stay with us always.'

Jenny's face fell. She might have made up her mind to tell him, but she hadn't done so yet. How could he spill the beans without her say-so? After all that guff about not hurting either of them, too. And where had idea that he was going to stay with them always come from? Oh, no.

He could think again on that one. Visits to Jamie were fine, but him live with them? Never!

Her mother must have seen her reaction and indicated with her head that they should have a word in the bedroom. When Jenny didn't move, she said, 'Jamie's so excited. He's been waiting to tell you.'

Jenny's steps were wooden as she moved over to Jamie and hugged him as she usually did when she arrived home. 'What a lovely surprise for you.'

Max watched her with apprehension. He knew her words meant it was a surprise to her as well, but not a lovely one. She was clearly furious that she hadn't been the one to tell Jamie, but what else could he have done?

'Are you all right with Jamie, Audrey, if Jenny and I pop downstairs for a drink?'

She nodded anxiously. 'No problem.'

The moment they reached the kitchen Jenny snapped, 'What the—' But Max slid a hand over her mouth to prevent her saying more until he had closed the door.

'Now, before you have a go at me, let me tell you what happened. Jamie was having his tea and was so excited that he came out with it out of the blue.'

'Came out with what, for goodness' sake? That he recognised the likeness between you? Very likely. Or—'

'Jenny, stop it.' His firm tone did the trick and she ceased her scathing tirade.

'What Jamie actually said was, "I do like you, Max. You're such fun. I wish you'd be my dad. I haven't got one."'

At Jenny's gasp he continued, 'I know you wanted to tell him when the time was right, and what better time could there have been to do it? It was the ideal opportunity.'

'Except that I wasn't there to share it.'

'So for your gratification you'd have preferred to do it when he might not have taken it so well? Come off it, Jenny. Jamie's the important one here, not you. And he accepted it as naturally as he possibly could have done.'

Startled by his unaccustomed rancour, Jenny grimaced. She was about to respond in kind when a sudden recollection of her fears for Max earlier in the afternoon changed her mind. 'You're right, of course. You'll make a great dad.'

He pulled her roughly into his arms, and when their cheeks brushed she realised he was crying. She put up a hand and wiped away the tears. 'I'm sorry, Max,' she said. 'That was selfish of me. All I can offer in mitigation is three years of making decisions about him on my own.'

He took her hand from his face and placed a kiss in the palm. 'Not any more, love. Not any more. I want to share in everything from now on.'

He held her slightly away from him then, and for endless seconds studied her face as if waiting for her reaction. But she was so confused as to what exactly he was asking of her that she couldn't answer.

'Oh, Jenny,' he murmured, and buried his face in her hair. 'What do I have to do to convince you?'

He lowered his head slowly, and as their lips met she could taste the saltiness of his tears.

His mouth moved on hers in the way she remembered so well, making her lose control of her senses sufficiently to respond—until she remembered his reaction the night she'd told him about Jamie. How could she believe he wasn't just doing this for Jamie's sake? And that wasn't what she wanted.

He tried to pull her back into his arms, and when she

resisted murmured, 'Why? Why, Jenny?' His bewilderment tore at her heartstrings as he asked again, 'Why? You obviously want me. We were so good together.'

'Maybe. But things have changed. I'm sorry, Max. This won't stop you seeing Jamie. You don't have to sleep with me to gain access.'

He winced. 'I'm talking about marriage, not—'

'I'm sorry, Max, but no. I must go and read to Jamie now. This is our special time together, after I've been at work, and it's important not to miss it today. He'll need to talk.'

Aware she was deliberately shutting him out, Max sank down into the nearest chair, unsure whether to leave before she finished the story or wait and attempt to reason with her.

Perhaps if she would agree to join him for a meal…?

Mrs Stalham came downstairs and told him with an apologetic smile, 'Jenny says she'll be a long time, so not to wait.'

'Even if I want to?'

'Give her time, Max. He's her whole life at the moment.'

Guessing she meant time to get used to sharing the care of Jamie, he nodded ruefully. 'If only she'd told me in the beginning.'

'She must have had a reason.' When he started to interrupt, she held up a hand. 'I don't want to know what happened between you. It's all in the past. But your appearance on the scene has brought everything back for Jenny. So, as I said, she needs time.'

'She still thinks I'm only interested in Jamie. Believe me, I came to Catonbury to try and find *her*, and at that time I didn't know he existed.'

'You need to say these things to Jenny. Not me. But not tonight. Let her simmer down and come to terms with Jamie's knowing about you. I know my daughter. If it's any consolation, I think you'd be good for them both. But I wouldn't dream of interfering.'

He crossed the room in a stride and gave her a warm hug. 'And you'd make a great mother-in-law.'

She led the way to the front door. 'Let's hope we both get a chance to find out, then. Whatever, we can keep in touch, because I know she won't stop you seeing Jamie. Not now.'

'Goodnight, Mrs Stalham. And thank you for everything. Including the tea.'

To Jenny's relief, Tuesday was a relatively quiet day, and she was able to catch up with the administrative work of the department. The only problem was that it allowed her too much time to think. After a restless night she still hadn't made her mind up how to handle her relationship with Max.

Apart from a brief greeting when she arrived in the department their paths hadn't crossed that morning. It was nearly lunchtime when he came to see if there was any coffee available.

'I'll make some,' she told him, and she dashed to the coffee machine in an attempt to avoid eye contact.

'No, Jenny. Please don't do that. I thought there might be a drop left in the jug. I've been to a planning meeting and their coffee would have been better for cleaning the drains.'

'It's no problem. I'd like another cup anyway.'

'As long as you're not doing it specially for me. I thought I'd go to lunch sooner rather then later. In case all hell is let loose this afternoon.'

She turned to agree that it was more than likely, but discovered he had gone. And without inviting her to lunch with him as he usually did when all was quiet. Her heart twisted painfully as she realised it was her own fault. She shouldn't have been so unreasonable the evening before, even though she'd been upset and disappointed at Jamie learning the news about Max when she wasn't there.

She'd been lucky so far, hadn't she? She'd had the privilege of sharing every milestone in her son's life while Max had not even known what he was missing. So why did she begrudge him that one opportunity to be a part of his son's life? It wasn't as if Jamie had been hurt by it.

She grimaced and started the primed coffee machine. Her behaviour had probably soured any enjoyment for him anyway, so she really couldn't blame him if their friendship was now a thing of the past. Though it wasn't what she had intended, and she certainly didn't want it if he was going to become involved in Jamie's care. For the boy's sake they needed to at least remain friends.

An hour later she decided to get some lunch and, discovering Rosie was already down there, made her way to the canteen to join her. She saw them the moment she walked through the door. At a table in the window corner, laughing together at some shared joke.

She turned on her heels and made her way back to the department.

Max joined her in the office as she was about to go off duty. 'You must be hungry by now.'

She frowned. 'Hungry?'

'You didn't have any lunch, did you? You must have had second thoughts when you saw what was on offer.'

'I'm surprised you noticed.'

'What do you mean by that?'

'You were too busy chatting with Rosie.'

'Ah! That's the second time you've accused me of being too busy and the second time you've been wrong.'

She didn't know what he was talking about, and wasn't about to ask.

'I came to ask if I could take Jamie to the local park on Saturday afternoon. They have a miniature steam locomotive there, giving rides. It's the last run this season.'

'Saturday? Alone?'

'You don't trust me, do you? He's my son as well, Jenny,' he told her gently, 'and I'd like to introduce him to some of the more masculine leisure pursuits.'

'But—but are they safe?'

'If properly controlled, and these are.'

'He's only three.'

'So will most of the other children having a ride be.'

'I don't remember you being interested in things like that when—when…' She faltered, unable to find the words to describe their short time together when Jamie was conceived.

'I don't find steam engines a riveting conversation during lovemaking.'

She felt the flush on her cheeks intensify. 'Except that love wasn't involved.'

'I think it was, Jen. Oh, yes! I certainly think it was.'

His eyes locked with hers, and she recognised he'd guessed what their brief affair had meant to her, so she hurried to tell him, 'If Jamie wants to go to the train track with you he can. I'll let you know tomorrow.' She checked her watch. 'I must get off home now. Make up for being so late last night.'

He raised an eyebrow, but made no comment and left her to hand over to Annette.

Jamie jumped at the chance of going with Max to the trains. When he got up on Saturday morning he was so excited that he couldn't eat his breakfast. By lunchtime Jenny had heard Max's name mentioned so many times that she was beginning to wish she'd never agreed. Or at least had offered to go with them. But it was too late now. He would think she didn't trust him.

When she called Jamie for his lunch he rushed in. 'Is Max here?'

'No,' she snapped, 'and if you don't eat every bit of your lunch he won't be coming.'

Jamie looked at her reproachfully and she felt instantly guilty. Why take it out on the boy? He barely spoke throughout the meal, and by the time he had finished eating she noticed his cheeks were flushed. 'Have you drunk all your juice?' she asked him.

He nodded eagerly and tipped his cup upside down to show her. A few drops of juice stained the cloth, but she said nothing but, 'Would you like some more?'

He shook his head. 'Can I get down now?'

'I'll just wipe your face over.' As she did so she felt his forehead, warm to the touch, and frowned. 'Do you feel OK, Jamie?'

'Yep. I'm going to ride on a train now,' he told her, for what seemed like the hundredth time that day.

By the time Max was due she was sure he was cooking up a raised temperature, and wondered if she ought to let him go. As she had expected, Max dismissed her fears. 'He's just over-excited. I won't keep him out too long anyway. We'll be back by four-thirty.'

Jenny couldn't settle to anything that afternoon. The minutes dragged, and if she checked her watch once, she did it at least every five minutes.

Four-thirty came and went with no sign of Max and

Jamie. At five o'clock she banged on the door of the annexe and poured out her fears to her mother.

'He's kidnapped him. I *knew* he just wanted Jamie.'

Her mother laughed shook her head. 'Don't be silly. He's not going to ruin his career doing something like that. Something's delayed them, that's all. Or Max has forgotten the time because they are enjoying themselves so much.'

'He could phone!'

'Don't you have his mobile number?'

'I don't think so. I could get it off Rosie.'

She dashed to the telephone, but only Rosie's answer machine greeted her.

Almost immediately it rang. She snatched up the receiver. 'Rosie—is that you?'

'No. It's Max.'

'Where are you? Where's Jamie? You promised—why aren't you back here?'

'Calm down, Jen. I'm ringing from the hospital.'

'The hospital? I knew those trains weren't safe. What's happened to him?' she screamed over the telephone, tears streaming down her face.

Her mother was beside her and placed a comforting arm around her.

'Jenny. Please keep quiet for a moment and listen. You need to come here immediately, but you are not to drive. Call a taxi. I think Jamie has meningitis.'

CHAPTER TEN

'M-MENINGITIS?' she stuttered. 'Oh, God, no. I'm on my way.' She dropped the receiver from her hand and demanded, 'Why, oh, why did I let him go?'

Her mother lifted it and said, 'Max? It's Audrey Stalham.'

There was a short silence and then her mother said, 'No. Jamie has no allergies. Has he, Jenny?' She turned to her daughter for confirmation.

Numbly Jenny shook her head.

He must have repeated his instructions then, as once the call was finished her mother ordered a taxi and helped Jenny to collect a bag together with Jamie's child health record and his favourite bedtime toy—a garish pink dog.

'Meningitis. Mum—I can't wait for the taxi.' She lifted her car keys.

Her mother caught her arm. 'Jamie needs you,' she told her daughter firmly. 'And so does Max. You have to be strong for them both. By the time you get his pyjamas the taxi will be here.'

'I knew he couldn't be trusted.'

'Don't talk rubbish.'

'Why didn't he call me earlier?'

'I expect he thought getting Jamie to hospital was more important.'

She couldn't argue with that, and rushed out to the taxi that had just arrived. 'The hospital. Quickly.' Her mother, who had stopped to secure the front door behind them, only just made it into the vehicle before it shot off.

When they arrived at the hospital Jenny was so distraught she could barely put one step in front of the other, and when she saw the concerned faces of her staff it was all she could do to whisper, 'Where is Jamie?'

Leanne took her to one of the resus rooms where John Harlow, the hospital paediatrician, was examining him after being called in by his own registrar. Jenny gasped at the sight of the tiny figure lying on the bed, attached to monitors and a slowly dripping infusion. It was so easy to be calm and professional about things when it wasn't your own child lying there.

She ran across to him and put the back of her hand on his hot cheek. Tears poured down her face as she murmured, 'Mummy's here, Jamie darling.'

'Jenny.' John Harlow acknowledged her quietly. 'We're still waiting for confirmation of the results of the lumbar puncture, but it's pretty definite it's Meningococcus B.'

'What does that mean?' she heard her mother ask Max, who was holding Jamie's hand on the far side of the trolley.

'We've taken a sample of fluid from around the spinal cord and we are testing it to see what bugs are causing Jamie's problems. I've just checked his vaccination record is up to date, so we know which one it's likely to be.'

Jenny smoothed the hair away from the boy's forehead and kissed him repeatedly. 'Mummy's here now, love.' Although he opened his eyes he showed no recognition.

'Has he had an antibiotic?' she demanded of no one in particular.

Max nodded and told her quietly, 'He had penicillin the moment we saw the turbid spinal fluid. If the diagnosis is confirmed Jamie's closest contacts will need to take a course of rifampicin.'

The consultant left to check with the children's ward, and the remainder of the team followed after telling Jenny and Max to ring if they were wanted.

'I'll be outside if you need me.' Her mother left as well, and Jenny knew she was deliberately leaving them alone.

She returned her attention to the boy, but when it was obvious there was nothing she could do for the moment but smooth his forehead she whispered, 'What exactly happened?'

Mac reached across and took hold of her free hand. 'We went on a train and Jamie loved it, but after the second ride he complained his head hurt. He still felt feverish, so I took him across to the park café for a squash. It was soon obvious he wasn't at all well. I was on my way back to the car to bring him home when he was sick, and I realised his condition was deteriorating rapidly. I checked and discovered that he had some neck stiffness so I brought him straight here.'

The tears she had been struggling to stem began to flow again. 'That's the second time this week that I haven't been there when he needed me,' she sobbed.

Max walked round the bed and put his arms around her. 'You can't be with him every moment of the day, Jen.'

She wasn't in a mood to be pacified and flared, 'I had been until you came on the scene.' She felt guilty that she hadn't been there, and yet she needed to blame someone and he was available. She reasoned that it must be all *his* fault. Jamie had had no problems until then.

'Jenny, Jenny,' he crooned softly. 'It's a bug. This would have happened wherever he was. I know you would have recognised the signs immediately, but so did I. He's having the best care possible.'

She rested her head on his shoulder and wept. He

smoothed the back of her head and cradled her in his arms until she started to calm down.

'They're going to move him up to the children's ward as soon as a bed's ready,' he told her quietly. 'You can stay with him there. Your mother, too, if that's what you would prefer?'

'I don't think that would be fair on her. She does enough already.'

'That's what I hoped you say,' he murmured into her hair, before kissing her warmly. 'I'll get Rosie to take her for a cup of tea and then run her home.'

'Rosie? Oh.' She clapped a hand to her mouth. 'I suppose the whole department must know about Jamie now. And that you're his father…'

'Is that such a bad thing, Jenny?'

When she didn't answer, he shrugged. 'I'm surprised you haven't told them about him long before this.'

She brushed away the worst of her tears. 'I didn't want to admit I was a single mum when I started here, and as you weren't around it didn't matter.'

'But you think it matters now?' he asked softly as she turned and placed a hand back on their son's hot forehead.

Unsure what to answer, she slid her hand under the cover and grasped Jamie's. What she saw on his momentarily exposed skin made her cry out in terror, 'Max— he's got spots. Look— Max, look.'

He didn't answer immediately, and she looked up to discover he wasn't looking at the spots but at her. And the distress she saw in his face could only mean one thing.

'It's a bad sign, isn't it?'

'Calm down, Jenny. We knew this was likely to happen.'

She clutched at his arm. 'But, Max, he could die. Or be brain-damaged. Or—'

'Stop meeting trouble halfway. He started treatment early in the development of the disease and that can only be a good sign. We have to be positive. For Jamie's sake. Come and have a cup of coffee.'

'I'm not leaving him, Max. I'm all he's got. He needs me here.' Max sighed when she added, 'You go and get one. I'm used to coping on my own.'

He released her abruptly, and after saying, 'I'll bring one through to you,' left the room.

She groaned as the door closed behind him. Why had she said that? All she'd meant was that he deserved one after the worry of what had happened, but she'd phrased it so badly. For someone renowned for her tact at work she seemed to have an unerring knack of saying the wrong thing to Max.

All she could do was apologise and explain when he came back with the coffee.

However, it was Fran who brought her tea, not coffee, and after she'd placed it beside Jenny she rested a sympathetic hand on her shoulder. 'He's in the best hands.'

'Thanks, Fran.'

'Anything else I can get you?'

Jenny shook her head and smiled. 'It's funny being on the receiving end of your reassurance.'

The girl coloured. 'He's a lovely boy.'

'Thanks.'

'It's no wonder Mr Field's so upset.'

Upset? And it was Jenny's fault. He'd done everything he possibly could for Jamie and she'd been so sunk in her own misery that she'd made him feel he wasn't wanted. But he was. He was Jamie's father, and although she wasn't prepared to make any kind of a commitment she had to admit the moment he'd left the room she'd felt bereft. As if a part of her was missing.

'Where is he?'

'He was in your office.'

'Could you stay a moment while I go and find him. Call me immediately if there's any change.'

The office door was closed and she pushed it open slowly. Max was on his own and looked up at her with reddened eyes.

She quickly closed the door and wrapped her arms around him. 'Why aren't you with us, Max? We need you.'

'Do you? What for? You've managed without me so far, and the first day I take him out he finishes up here.'

'But that's not your fault, Max. You said yourself, it's a bug. He needs his father.'

'A father you don't trust and you're ashamed to admit to.'

'Max.' She was horrified. 'That's not true.'

'Isn't it? I think your refusal to answer my questions made it quite clear in there that you'd be happier if your colleagues didn't know I was Jamie's father.'

She covered her face with both her hands and groaned. 'Max, that was the last thing I meant... Max, please come back. I don't want to be alone with him.'

'I'll arrange for your mother to stay with you. For one night at least.'

It wasn't her mother she wanted. It was Max. She tightened her arms around him. She felt safe with him. As if everything would be all right if only she could stay cradled against the firm muscles of his chest, listening to the regular beating of his heart. She knew at that moment that, however he felt about her, she didn't want to face what might happen without him. 'Please stay, Max. Please.'

'As his father? Or as a doctor? Which is it, Jen? I need to know.'

'As his father, Max,' she whispered.

'What about us,' he murmured into her hair.

'Us?'

'You know how I feel about you, Jen.'

Oh, yes, she knew all right—and that was the problem. 'We're friends, aren't we? Come on, now. I don't think we ought to leave *our* son on his own any longer.' She deliberately emphasised the 'our'. 'They'll be moving him soon.'

He gave her a despairing look and said, 'You go up to the ward with him. I'll follow in a moment.'

'Come now, Max,' she pleaded.

He shook his head. 'I have things to do. I won't be long.'

She was pleased when he joined her almost immediately, bringing with him the fresh smell of the soap he'd used to wash his face.

'Any change?' he asked.

She shook her head and he took a seat on the opposite side of the bed.

The next thirty-six hours were the longest Jenny could ever remember. Jamie's condition didn't change, and although Max was there for much of the time he was remote, as if they were strangers. Which she supposed they were.

The next morning he told her it was a good sign that Jamie's condition wasn't deteriorating, but Jenny knew it wasn't improving, either. She stayed at the hospital the whole time and slept very little. Her mother visited a couple of times and tried to persuade her to take a break, but Jenny refused.

Max tried to carry on with his usual routine, but the remainder of the A & E staff did their best to cover for him so he could spend as much time with Jamie as possible. All he could do was be there for him—and his mother—if they needed him.

They were rarely left alone long. An endless of stream of doctors and nurses checked and rechecked Jamie's condition, and did everything that was necessary to promote his recovery.

It was only when his fever eased and he drank a few sips of water that they dared to hope that he was going to make it.

'How's your head, old son?' Max asked him tenderly the next time he woke.

Jamie raised a hand to his temple and muttered groggily, 'Still there.' Jenny giggled for the first time Max could remember since his arrival at the hospital, and he thought it the most delicious sound. He reached across and squeezed her hand.

From that moment the rapport between them improved daily. Max thought it was probably a subconscious act on both their parts, for Jamie's benefit, but he didn't care. He was enjoying their time together and he was sure Jenny was, too. It gave him hope for the future.

It was several days later, when Jamie was much better and his grandmother was reading him a book, when he said quietly to Jenny, 'Enough's enough. I'm going to take you home for a good meal, a good rest and a good talk.'

'Sounds wonderful,' she said. 'We'll be back in a couple of hours,' she told Jamie.

As they scurried out of the ward, like a couple of children escaping from control, they were stopped by a beaming Mrs Hobson.

'I'm taking Kyle home today. All thanks to you, Sister.

His dad has moved in with that Sharon, and so they've agreed I can keep Kyle with me. They'll be round tomorrow to see how we're doing.'

'I'm so pleased to hear it.' Jenny was embarrassed by her effusive thanks.

'I hear your little lad's much better as well. I'm so glad. They wouldn't let me come and bother you before this.'

Jenny nodded and smiled. 'He's going to be fine. And so are you. Look after Kyle, won't you?'

Mrs Hobson nodded, her chest swelling with pride. 'They said Kyle was well looked after apart from the injuries. No offence meant, Sister, but I hope I don't see you again. Not here, anyway.'

'I couldn't agree more,' Jenny smiled.

As they made their way to the car park Max said, 'She's not going to have it easy. Especially as Kyle will be susceptible to every infection going now they've had to remove his spleen. But you know, I think she'll cope.'

'Like all single mothers have to.'

He nodded, tempted to say that *she* didn't have to be one any longer, but he decided to wait until they reached the house.

It seemed strange to be out in the fresh air after so many days closeted in the hospital, and Jenny felt happy. Happier than she had for a long time. And she knew she had Max to thank for that. He was great company and hadn't been able to do enough for both her and Jamie during the past few days.

After she'd unlocked the door she turned to him and impulsively kissed him. 'Thanks for all you've done, Max. Are you coming in?'

'I thought you'd never ask.' He grinned, sweeping her up into his arms and carrying her across the threshold.

When he eventually finished kissing her, he set her back on her feet and closed the door.

She swallowed hard and said, 'I thought that custom was for newly weds.'

'Not necessarily. New beginnings. The start of married life. The start of a new phase in our relationship. What's the difference?'

'I hear what you're saying, Max, and I couldn't be happier the way things are between us at the moment—as long as you understand that I'm not going to marry you. I've come to terms with the fact that you don't love me, and I'm perfectly happy for us to be friends. Just not married. I've seen enough of loveless unions to know it's a mistake.'

He sighed and shook his head. 'That old chestnut again. Who says I don't love you, Jenny Stalham?'

'Your mother.'

'My mother?' His eyes locked with hers for endless seconds. 'You mentioned her before and I meant to ask when you'd met her.'

'Oh, I haven't met her. Just talked to her on the telephone when I rang to tell you I was pregnant. She made it clear that Clare was the love of your life and—'

'You phoned me? At home? Jenny, I had no idea—'

'I left a couple of messages—one with my new number here.'

'She never— Did you tell her you were pregnant?'

'You must be joking—when she'd just told me that the moment Clare was better you would set the wedding date?'

'I had no idea you left your new number for me. I had to beg your friends at Rexford to get it.'

'Beg? But—but you never bothered to ring.'

'Oh, but I did. I wasn't sure if I should when your

colleagues at Rexford told me you'd left to be with your—your fiancé, I believe they called him. Especially after you'd been so distant when I rang the night before your interview.'

She swallowed hard. 'I remember that night—I was sure I was pregnant but I didn't want to say anything until I'd done a test. I was terrified, Max. Terrified you'd run when you heard the news. All I could think about was carrying your baby and I don't know what to say to you.'

He hesitated. 'When I heard you'd gone I thought you hadn't wanted to tell me to my face that you had someone else. But I did ring, Jenny,' he rushed on to say. 'And I spoke to…' He stopped as realisation dawned. 'I thought I must be speaking to the new man in your life—but now you tell me there wasn't one. So why did whoever it was tell me so firmly you wanted nothing more to do with me?'

She groaned. 'My father, I'll bet. He thought the world of me, and I suppose he thought he was protecting me from being hurt again. I can't believe it. He never even told me you rang…'

He let out a delighted roar of laughter. 'I don't believe this. I love you, Jenny Stalham. With all my heart. Always have. Always will. You do believe me, don't you?' Suddenly serious, he told her, 'I've always wanted to take care of you, and now Jamie. For ever. Why do you think I came to look for you?'

He enveloped her in a bear hug and rained kisses on her lips, her cheeks, wherever he could reach. Even on her closed eyelids. When she could get her breath back, she said, 'Whatever our parents may have decided?'

Solemnly he took both her hands in his. 'Whatever. Because we've wasted too much time already. I love you so much, Jenny, and I'm pretty sure you love me. Don't you?' His voice was barely a whisper.

'Yes, I do, Max. But—'

'Jenny, that's all I want to hear.' He hugged her to him and swung her round the room. 'I think parent power zapped us both. But we'll show them. I think I've won your mother over already.'

'I can believe that—so why did you take so long to convince me?'

He kissed her gently. 'Perhaps because of Jamie? I can understand that.' Tears sprang to her eyes as he said, 'Do you think we'll be as bad as that when our children grow up?'

'Our *children*, did you say?'

'Yes. Do you think we'll be as bad?'

Completely dazed by the turn their conversation had taken, she shook her head. 'Did you say children?'

'I think that's the only way we're going to avoid inflicting the curse of the only child on Jamie. And if we're going to be back at the hospital within the two hours you promised we ought to get started on it right away.' He held her to him in a crushing embrace.

Her heart pounding in her chest, she told him happily, 'I don't know what you're suggesting, Max Field.' But her fingers were giving the lie to her words as they slid down from his broad shoulders to unbutton his fancy waistcoat.

'Steady on.' He quickly rescued his watch from the pocket. 'Careful. This is a valuable heirloom. As my legitimate first son, Jamie will have it one day.'

'Legitimate?'

'I think we should fix our wedding the moment Jamie is well enough to officiate as a page boy. Don't you agree?'

The knowledge that he really had loved her all along had dispersed all her doubts, and she told him quietly, 'I think Jamie would like that.'

'And his mother?'

'She thinks she's the luckiest woman in Catonbury.' She pulled his face down to hers so that she could kiss him. 'She'd prove it to you if it wasn't time to get back.' She pointed to the watch he had laid on the table. 'Sorry, Max, but you might as well get used to it. This is the way it's going to be for the next twenty years! At least. Our son needs us.'

Modern Romance™
...seduction and
passion guaranteed

Tender Romance™
...love affairs that
last a lifetime

Sensual Romance™
...sassy, sexy and
seductive

Blaze™
...sultry days and
steamy nights

Medical Romance™
...medical drama on
the pulse

Historical Romance™
...rich, vivid and
passionate

27 new titles every month.

With all kinds of Romance for
every kind of mood...

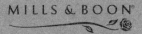

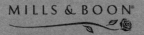

Don't miss *Book Two* of this BRAND-NEW 12 book collection 'Bachelor Auction'.

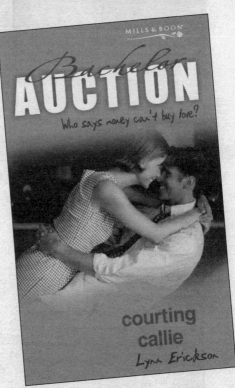

Who says money can't buy love?

On sale 4th October

FREE

2 BOOKS
AND A SURPRISE GIFT!

We would like to take this opportunity to thank you for reading this Mills & Boon® book by offering you the chance to take TWO more specially selected titles from the Medical Romance™ series absolutely FREE! We're also making this offer to introduce you to the benefits of the Reader Service™—

- ★ FREE home delivery
- ★ FREE monthly Newsletter
- ★ FREE gifts and competitions
- ★ Exclusive Reader Service discount
- ★ Books available before they're in the shops

Accepting these FREE books and gift places you under no obligation to buy; you may cancel at any time, even after receiving your free shipment. Simply complete your details below and return the entire page to the address below. **You don't even need a stamp!**

YES! Please send me 2 free Medical Romance books and a surprise gift. I understand that unless you hear from me, I will receive 4 superb new titles every month for just £2.55 each, postage and packing free. I am under no obligation to purchase any books and may cancel my subscription at any time. The free books and gift will be mine to keep in any case.

M2ZEC

Ms/Mrs/Miss/Mr ....Initials ....
BLOCK CAPITALS PLEASE

Surname ....

Address ....

....

....Postcode ....

Send this whole page to:
UK: FREEPOST CN81, Croydon, CR9 3WZ
EIRE: PO Box 4546, Kilcock, County Kildare (stamp required)